+ hugs—
Zigs

HISTORICAL
INACCURACIES

HISTORICAL INACCURACIES

Zig Zag Claybourne

Also by Clarence Young:

By All Our Violent Guides

God, Quiet Spaces, Twentieth Century News

Two Brothers: Poems from the Basement

Neon Lights (as Zig Zag Claybourne)

HISTORICAL INACCURACIES

Contents

"I can see Russia from my house,"
Sarah Palin never said.

Even Beelzebub needs to be accurately quoted.

SHORT STORIES

Prehistoric Jesus didn't work out. Premature transfiguration. Inquisition Jesus kept slipping on the blood. No traction, no peace. Sitcom Jesus had all the right ingredients but wasn't funny enough for anyone to want to buy the entire first season on DVD. And why they thought to put an annoying kid in the cast no one knows. Tomorrow we'll have Techno Jesus. Tomorrow is today.

Memory was ragged and sinful, so she closed her eyes and tried not to remember. Heavy breathing around her meant she was the only one awake again. She stretched flat and forced the coarse frock into a straight line across her knees. Sister Patricia taught the meditative state as being the closest to grace. She completed the meditative posture, being perfectly smooth, perfectly straight, hands clasped atop her belly.

The Inquisitors were to arrive at first bell. Inspection was to take place immediately. Guarded whispers announced the Inquisitors' abilities to sense the sinful thoughts. Numerous disappearances corroborated this.

Voletta doubled her efforts to erase the thought: Father Nacio's arm creating a bustle of Sister Nicita's habit as his hand traveled upward. Sister Nicita was known to have sensitive skin and was permitted a lesser amount of necessary clothing. She was a quiet woman who preferred tending manuscripts and scrolls over engaging others, creating a soil about her perfect for maliciousness. It was even mentioned among the initiates that a sole layer of undergarments kept her from being bare, and at times not even that.

A sharp snore interrupted the memory. Gordita's passages were obstructed again.

Voletta rolled quietly off her cot. The large girl could go nearly a minute without breathing before a powerful suck of air forced its way through the folds of her neck to restart her lungs. Once restarted, Gordita engaged in an hour long display of variable snoring, which was an hour Voletta couldn't afford to have taken from her, not tonight. By now she had Gordita trained. Gordita was too large for her to move by herself, but over the last few months she'd trained her to respond like a horse to taps and nudges. She poked Gordita quickly in the ribs. Gordita's body responded away from the poke. On her side, she tended to snore less.

Only people of higher breeding were allowed to know precisely when the Inquisitors' ship was to port. For all she knew it might be moored now with several Inquisitors steadfastly scourging themselves to increase the breadth and depth of their psychic probing.

She quickly lay flat again, legs together, hem straight, hands clasped, prayer fervent, and mind...mind running straight for that image. Father Nacio's hand clearly traveled the contours of Sister Nicita's calf with the calm disposition of a man about his given business. He went far enough on the frozen and stony sister as she descended the small ladder from returning *D'Amato's Instrucciones* to the shelves that a pinch of her pale white thigh was visible, and at that point Voletta secretly rushed herself from the library cellar where girls who bled were encouraged to go. She was already sixteen and had only bled twice. Even Gordita was a regular bleeder, had been doing so for years, she said. It was the expulsion of sin.

Father Nacio regularly conducted business among the servants. It was deserved and accepted. The expulsion of sin, which every great man was due in order that they remain great, was no shame among men, for men had the concerns of the entire world. The kitchen girls in particular, where it was hot and humid and they thought nothing of bare arms or undone laces and tended to have the smell of food about them—food being well known to incite lust; it was why initiates ate only breads, meal porridge and dried meat—it was accepted that conduct with kitchen girls was much the same as needing to urinate or having additional hands to help with the ringing of the Abbey's massive bell.

The sisters, on the other hand, were holy. God willing, Voletta would become one herself. It was what all initiates hoped for, those who weren't favorably bred to that station. She shared bare quarters with forty others. Of those, eight were likely to rise and the others would replace the aging as permanent fixtures inside the Abbey walls, either in the kitchens or as washerwomen. The sisters stressed that beauty was God's work. Voletta's face was plain, her body unremarkable. Her breasts were too large but she did her best to flatten them. But there were many more homely than she. She was indentured to the Abbey until such time as she rose to sisterhood and blessed piety. If not, being poor, she belonged with the stable, another proper mount in the service of her betters.

But the image of Sister Nicita's pale thigh would not leave her mind.

And there was so little left of this night.

The ship docked in the morning, announcing itself only by those smaller vessels that scurried away from it. It bore no flags or banners save one purple flag at the keel as warning to pirates to make their peace before attacking. The presence of Inquisition ships in these waters had cut piracy considerably, except upon those ships Inquisition schooners deemed heretic and were thus expected to tithe their cargo and possessions to the church as penance.

Had the initiates been allowed, they would have witnessed a funereal debarkation. Only one of the Inquisitors was old, but all moved with the slow gait of others' time. Each man's head excruciatingly scanned the surroundings between steps, left to right, right to left, in actuality seeing nothing with the impression of seeing all.

Fathers Nacio and Banquesas bowed to greet them.

"Eminences. God brings you to us favorably."

Inquisitor Jauregio touched the Father briefly on the forehead. The three other Inquisitors were arrayed behind him. They made no similar move.

Father Banquesas had hurt his knee a day earlier and was slow to position himself.

"Father Banquesas, will you not give us your thoughts?"

"Of course, Eminence," the old friar said, stumbling in haste. "Infirmities," he added.

"Infirmities," said the Inquisitor, "have damned legions who do not face them as men."

The Father dropped awkwardly and painfully to one knee. He bowed his head without response. The Inquisitor's touch at his forehead was so brief it hardly seemed worth the pain but Banquesas bore it and, as the three slowly marched on, refused Father Nacio's assistance with a curt gesture of his hand, the old fool. What greater sin was pride before your betters, particularly in obeisance of some silly ruse? Father Nacio took up step behind the Inquisitors and prayed that Banquesas' gesture went unnoticed.

The damp saltiness of the coastline tended to leave permanent frowns on the faces of anyone spending lifetimes there. The Fathers were aware of this. Nacio regularly visited the port town for prayer missions, a relic of his younger days that most older clergy had long given up. The sea shriveled things, flesh and souls equally, until residents stared at the living with the same flat, dead eyes as a fish, precisely the way the local coachman watched the Inquisitors slowly approach and be methodically assisted aboard by the three invisible young men always with them; particularly the way the coachman regarded Father Nacio. Father Nacio's prayers over his daughter had given him the grandson back home tending the stables.

Two of the young men took up posts on either side of Javier, the coachman. The third attached to the coach at the rear. They were not Spaniards, those three, and that was no great observation. All three were as black as soot with the tight, gaunt skin of warriors. Javier's flat stare bumped blindly against the hard set of one's jaw, then proceeded on, neither man giving evidence of life. They were two miles from Lagro Abbey and it was humid. The omnipresent grey sky suffocated them as the coachman lightly whipped the horses, and continued to as the carriage hobbled along without breeze.

After the great bell rang out signaling the coach was halfway there, the Abbey came to sudden life with a swirl of washerwomen, cooks, initiates and groundsmen, moving all so efficiently that there was no sense of rushing, no cries of "Watch!" or "Hurry on!" The truth was there was never a moment when the Abbey wasn't in motion. It was a city unto itself outside the port town. The nearness of the Inquisitors simply meant rather than do two things do three. Father Nacio had instructed them under pain of sin that the Abbey show not a single thing out of place or person out of duty. Pains of sin were delivered by the Brotherhood, and delivered thoroughly. The Brotherhood were young men who themselves aspired to the wholesale deliverance of prayers to those most in need.

Doctrine did not allow the Sisters in the presence of the Inquisitors unless actively sought, and so all the sisters were shut in their rooms. Voletta had always imagined them fervently praying for the eradication of desires and sin.

The initiates lined the courtyard inside the Abbey's stocky grey entrance, a straight line of forty awkward girls in brown frocks and slippers stretching end to end. A light wind curled at their ankles.

Fathers Sifuentes and Benel kept ranks with a glance or a frown.

"Voletta, have you forgotten your place?"

"No, Father."

"Eyes down."

"Yes, Father."

"You do not speak," Benel reminded all, "unless spoken to. You are worthless young girls, unwashed and unformed."

Each girl made the sign of penitence over her forehead.

Father Benel's crows-feet deepened in satisfaction. He was a man given to smiling only when necessary. The Inquisitors would look favorably upon this line.

Presently there came a chorus of soft voices from outside the walls. The Brothers had begun their prayers of thanks for the divine works of the Inquisition. The coach passed the Brothers without pause. Porthos, who had taken the reins from the coachman the final quarter of their journey, stopped the coach just inside the Abbey's gates.

The three black warriors, Porthos, Athos and Aramis, jumped lithely as one, hands nowhere near swords yet always seeming so.

They strode directly to Father Sifuentes. This took a moment, as the Fathers were some thirty yards away. The coach remained locked.

The Fathers had no intention of speaking to slaves.

Athos spoke first.

"Why are these women here?"

"We thought the Eminences would like to see them."

"Do the Eminences need to see the stones?"

"No."

Father Benel tried speaking up. "It is customary..." Aramis' stare of open disbelief that this man was speaking stopped him.

"There are no customs that you know of," Athos said, eyes as flat as the coachman's. He had seen too much of the sea himself. "There is only what we tell you."

The warriors glanced left, right and seemingly through the stone of the Abbey itself. Athos turned on his heel and returned to the coach. Porthos and Aramis remained. They were dressed in the finest of ruffles and lace, which rendered them even more alien to the pauper Abbey.

The first of the Inquisitors exited. Had he stepped upon the backs of men to crawl him forward it would not have altered his permanent expression of expectancy one bit. This was Inquisitor Jauregio, and he was Death.

The next, Hell, was Inquisitor Boniface, the eldest of the group.

Power, the third, was wrapped in the fat of Inquisitor De Vega's jowls, a man who ate very little but seemed to gain twice as much as an ordinary man. A defect of nature, it was decided, brought on by a sinful mother.

The fourth Inquisitor was Murder. The ground moaned in pain as he stepped down.

Porthos and Aramis took up positions between Fathers Benel and Sifuentes and the Inquisitors.

Voletta had spent all night in prayer and meditation, willing herself to deny her random thoughts as ungodly with all due passion. The hairs her hands had rested atop had sent shivers through her skin. Each time she was slow in pushing memory away she itched shamefully.

Sunlight never seemed to follow Father Nacio. Even on a cloudy day like this it seemed darker directly around him.

He was cruel to all initiates but only in that initiates were meant to be treated cruelly. Their poverty had already damned them; redemption was much like slapping a dirty cloth against stone and twisting it dry until every drop of filthy water had been wrung out.

Voletta trembled. An itch of fear tingled her leg. But it was blood.

She froze. Everything solidified, and had time been hers to use she would have bent it into itself. Even if she had felt the wadded cloths absorbing all they could hold, she would not have been allowed to leave. The slow descent was a slug torturously wandering.

The Inquisitors stopped, spoke about coffers between Fathers Nacio and Sifuentes, then broke away into equidistant points along the line of initiates, scanning each girl slowly.

Hell (Inquisitor Boniface) stopped directly in front of Voletta.

"Give me your thoughts, girl."

She prayed for Father Nacio and Sister Nicita and begged forgiveness as the old man's finger made way to her head and touched her once, quickly.

"Bring her," he said to the wind and moved off. Fathers Nacio, Benel and Sifuentes remained a pace away. Father Banquesas remained on the outskirts, still near the coach, where he hoped to be forgotten.

Voletta was prepared to panic as the image of Nacio's burrowing hand burst full upon her. She gritted her teeth and kept her eyes down, and surprisingly felt a momentary speckle of defiance. The memory was hers but the deed was not.

All she saw of Hell were his feet.

The other Inquisitors made similar choices but did not limit themselves to one. Boniface ambled closer to his brethren. The slave in the brightest whites and reds Voletta had ever seen took the Inquisitor's place before her, staring at her chest a moment even as she pretended not to chance her peripheral view of him. She had never seen a black before. She knew they existed, but to see one here further convinced her of her damnation.

Under the damning stare of the warrior, her reactionary defiance shriveled immediately.

The initiates were just as immediately forgotten. The Inquisitors entered Lagro Abbey pulling along a train of guards, Fathers, Brothers and clerics.

Fathers Benel and Banquesas remained. Apparently the job had fallen to them to corral the initiates picked for questioning.

They barked names abruptly. Each girl stepped forward. None spoke a word. None looked up.

They prayed for forgiveness.

The Inquisitors' chambers were meant to conduct the deeper works of salvation, and so were built apart from the Abbey itself. A thick-walled rectangular building divided into four large cells, those four divided by half again, it was never used, never entered.

Just as evening fell Porthos completed his inspection of Voletta, keeping careful eye on her hands tied above her head. There had been occasions when slipped hands created suddenly fearless women. She was naked. The red clot of cloths lay on a rough table.

"Has she finished bleeding?"

"She has, Lord."

"Is she otherwise clean?"

Porthos nodded.

"The scar?" Hell asked her.

"My father, Lord," she murmured.

"An otherwise lovely back. Strong. Useful."

Porthos stoked the nearby fire with the point of his sword.

"Give her drink for the pain."

The sad, hard face opened a port of wine and dropped a small amount of laudanum in it from a pouch on a belt.

"I beg your mercy, Lord!" said Voletta.

The Inquisitor's attention was caught by a sill spider frantically wrapping up its prey; he offered up a distracted grunt to Voletta's entreaty.

She openly cried. "I beg mercy."

Porthos held a cup to her lips. She dutifully drank. The liquid was bitter but effervescent and she could tell as it traveled her innards that it was designed to change her. There was an intelligence to it.

"I beg mercy," she sobbed again.

"You beg which does not exist. Burn her there," the old man directed. "If you cry out—"

But it was too late. Porthos turned and grazed her with the tip of the blade. The chubby fold above her hip reddened violently. Voletta screamed.

"Be thrice damned!" screamed the old man back. "You will hold your sins and atone for them!" He sat in a seat directly behind her. "Receive her."

Porthos's eyes deadened. He took a vial from his pouch and approached her, pouring oil into his hand. He wedged the hand through her thighs and cupped her, slathering the oil through flesh and hair while muttering the sacrament in Latin for his and her ears alone, then an even softer word in a language she had never heard. It was Bantu for 'solitude.'

"Receive this vessel as thy lord and master," Hell commanded.

Sex was no secret. On more than one occasion before her call to the Abbey she had seen her father behind women when she dragged from the fields to hang her scythe in the shed. The women usually wore bored expressions whereas father's facial contortions gave the impression of agony.

"It hurts men," her mother had said, explaining her father's actions. "It's why he has to do it much, to deaden the pain. Life is tiresome between their legs, girl."

She remembered feeling the deepest pity for her father.

The black turned the wheel to lower the rope enough for her to bend under his calloused hand's direction. He was about to grip her pale thighs to spread them when she did it for him.

"Forgive me," she told him, craning her neck so he would see the sincerity of her plea. She pictured the last face she'd ever seen in front of her father, Estrella, whose heavy breasts pushed out of her blouse to slap at the air: one eyebrow shared between two eyes, jowls that swung forward with each of her father's thrusts, and the glance from the woman into Voletta's eyes that communicated merely *Oh, it's you.*

This was the expression she would adopt, dead, patient and sympathetic of...

Pain. Porthos entered quickly, causing her to scream with eyes wide open. She tried twisting off him. He grabbed her at the waist and tugged her, keeping her footing unbalanced. He reached for the vial of oil and emptied it at the small of her back. It waterfalled to coat his member, which, being foreign and dark, had to be the cause of Voletta's pain. Their flesh was incompatible.

She cried for them both.

Hell sat silently, neither gleeful nor hardened, merely omnipresent. Inquisitor Boniface knew men well and gauged Porthos perfectly. At the critical moment he rose from his seat, raised up the sleeve of his robe, and gripped Porthos's slick penis, which the Bantu had dutifully withdrawn.

Boniface closed his hand on it hard. The Bantu grunted. "Have you expelled your seed?" He squeezed again. Boniface tugged him forward, clumsily directing the penis' return to Voletta, who shivered uncontrollably. "Do you take pleasure from beasts, child?" The old hand remained trapped between them with Porthos' tight thrusts. Fear made the tips of her breasts hard. The old man took note of this.

"The touch of this thing excites you, and you seek mercy?" Boniface came around to cup her chin with his wet hand and raised her gaze to his. She clamped her eyes shut. Boniface smiled. "The sisterhood has no place for harlotry. Abase yourself."

Her ragged voice merged with Porthos' thumps. "Sister Nicita, forgive me! Father Nacio!"

Hell looked at his hand, sticky and tinged red. The overpowering human scent coming off it enraged him.

"Abase yourself until you are worthy of our Lord's consideration!"

This continued for three days. She was cleaned, fed, and slept tethered. She was raped depending on Hell's schedule, during the early day, perhaps after being left alone hours at a time, perhaps during the night. The remembered expressions of Lupita, Avril, Estrella and Jacinta with her father behind them in the far corner of the old shed became the only mirrors by which she knew her face.

Her memory had brought this upon her. Her thoughts pulled from her. She knew that. The Inquisitor's endurance was testament to both his faith and sacrifice. She would emerge cleansed by this and freed from the shameful lust Sister Nicita's pale flesh engendered. Voletta's imagination on that cot surrounded by snorers had transformed Father Nacio's hand into her own a dozen times over. She had imagined the placid acceptance of that thigh welcoming her even though she hadn't meant to; unintention alone accounted for the Inquisitor's leniency.

On the third day Inquisitors Boniface, De Vega, Jauregio and Xochiel discussed the final shipments of gold from Lagro Abbey. On that day Voletta was joined by another initiate whose thoughts must have been as impure and treacherous as her own. It was Zuce, who tended to speak very little and never needed an excuse to look down. She, too, was overly buxom, particularly due to her small stature. Voletta, from her tether in the center of the room, watched the girl being stripped, splashed in the face and body, then roughly dried. Voletta no longer saw Porthos. It was as though a ghost tended Zuce's ministrations. Voletta's mouth itself was open, gaping like a fish, an unconscious reaction to the humid stench that congealed in her nostrils. Porthos and his seed had marked her. She had never realized sex had a smell all its own. A marker of sin.

Everything that happened to Zuce happened without a single word between the Lord Inquisitor and his ghost, but the two men moved as an efficient unit. Inquisitor Boniface personally laid hands upon the girl, his member so swollen Voletta only dully imagined the pain he must be going through on Zuce's behalf. When the old man entered her his eyes shut as if burned, and where his fingernails dug into Zuce's sides there were clearly red welts. Voletta's eyes stared flatly the entire ordeal as Inquisitor Boniface debased himself to find the righteousness inside Zuce Pilanques. During indoctrination at the Abbey initiates were repeatedly instructed that righteousness is never lost, only buried. The acts of men require evil for evil, sacrifice to the good, and penance for every waking hour. None but his Excellency the King was more highly favored in God's eyes than his earthly arm of avenging angels, the Inquisitors. Inquisitors risked damnation with every contact with lower souls. She did not realize that tears came from her eyes and fell on the forearm she used as a pillow. They tracked the side of her face and itched, but they itched another person, a soul of base desires even now still being cleansed as she watched Inquisitor Boniface beat Zuce about the head and grab her hair in the manner of reining an unrelenting horse. Zuce yelped with the pain of the tug. The prayer she had just begun aloud was cut off before the first completed syllable.

"You will not speak," said Boniface close at her ear. "You are not fit to speak."

Zuce bit down, squeezed her eyes shut to the point where it hurt, and remained that way. Yet water finds a way. Tears rimmed her lashes and were refreshed each time robust thumps shook droplets free.

"Untie her hands. Turn her. Take me in your hands and release the devil you hold so dear." But Zuce had no idea what to do.

"My Lord?" she said with cracked voice.

He grabbed her about the head, fingers digging through her hair, causing her to panic.

"I have no further thoughts, Lord! Mother of God, forgive me!"

"Take me in your hands," he roared. She gripped the only thing pointing accusingly at her. "Do you tend your sins as though infants? Seek forgiveness!" She tugged. His eyes closed. Voletta followed his lead and prayed as well.

Eventually Voletta fell asleep. When she awoke Zuce was not there. Other initiates came to her during the night. Like theirs, her hands were now free. Because Voletta had been singled out first, they huddled their naked bodies close to her, mindful of their individual injuries but needing the solidarity of contact.

Brothers came for them during the night. They tended the initiates' wounds in silence, bathing and dressing them. They instructed them to speak to no one and returned them to their barracks. The girls returned to hard, uncomfortable beds, sliding atop their assigned spaces. Early bell announced the next morning. Amnesia assumed its post for all. Initiates performed their chores. Recited liturgies and meditative prayers were reinforced. The Fathers were looked after, as befitted those charged with the betterment of the flock.

The Inquisitors' ship, having departed at first light, left no more impression on Puerto Cielo Pescador than the time it took water to fill its place. The port's offerings went to the Abbey, the Abbey gave this to the Inquisition, and there was never need to prolong relations between the two. Port Pescador was acquainted with the wages of sin.

All knew that following every day, came the night.

Expletive Deleted

I had no idea what to do when a man surrendered. David seemed to though; he never lost his focus. I chanced a glance at Edric; he wasn't freaking. We were in a war, my country f***ing with their country, they whoever they are. It's not as if we know. It was hot, it was cold, it rained every day, we were plagued by locusts, there was strange s**t everywhere, and we were not men. The plants didn't look like our plants and the air smelled. We knew not to think beyond the day.

Myers was telling us the best way to f**k the president. That's when they tried to ambush us with amateur guerilla tactics straight off a half-assed newscast. We immediately flanked them and decided they were dead. Dead the way that's more than dead, like most folks won't die. It got quiet once the reports died. A man jumped out with his hands beating his head like he couldn't catch hold of it. Big dark hands like mine. He screamed something because our guns were pointed at him, and two people shot him. Two more like him jumped forward, arms raised toward some high god, crying and swallowing and putting their hands on their heads. They were saying clearly, suddenly, and insistently in a language everyone on the planet recognizes that it doesn't matter. This is not real. The fact that they were trying to kill us, trying very hard--because we were killing them too, very hard-- was not as important as we thought. Everything was all right. Anything you could get a time out on had to be all right.

Surrender, huh? Hands on heads, huh?

Bodies, bits and whole, lay scattered on uneven ground, interred later by wild dogs.

Our medic muttered something religious but I don't think he meant it. The two standing were in panic-blink mode and they breathed so hard I stopped breathing. They trembled. Somebody almost lowered his weapon but Myers screamed one word at him and it raised right up. Those two with dirty hands were the most dangerous people alive because they were alive. Eight bodies around, between and under our feet. I knew I was standing on a finger but couldn't move. You didn't shift.

I needed very much to shoot something, something that would create a memory in me and I'd remember till I was old or crazed, that would scab over my life except this one memory. The toy soldiers had died so quickly I couldn't recall a single one of them. I even tried to imagine them getting on a bus. I couldn't know how many my random bullets had gotten. There are no marksmen in war. If they're standing over there and you're standing over here, you point in their direction and pull the trigger. You try to pull it faster than the speed of light but the gun makes the rules. That's physics.

No mathematicians in war. Just metallurgy students.

I squeezed inside. My trigger. Squeezed it at these men confusing me. The metal pointed the right way, away from us and toward them. Anthony squeezed. Harkness squeezed. David squeezed. Those two, by rights, should not have been standing, because everybody squeezed at them. They were gibbering away, telling us their life story with words that didn't mean anything at all.

Corporal Myers said, "Down!" with his gun leveled and he squeezed but forgot to use his inside voice.

The one on the left tottered a step back; arms flailed before he went down like a wrecked kite. His backpack kept him suspended off the ground. It would have been funny on TV.

From eleven toy soldiers only one alive now, which made it weirder watching him standing pissing himself, arms akimbo. M**********r had just been trying to murder us.

We were just supposed to stop?

Corporal Myers turned away and dropped to his knees. Some part of him knew there was no future. He had been here forever. He would fight here forever.

Nobody wanted to keep squeezing inside. Myers jumped to his feet, ran a step toward the last man and whipped dirt in his face but the guy was too scared to flinch. Brains never save a man, fear does. "F**k y'all!" Myers shouted at him. He looked at each of us in turn. We were his. His men. And men know. We know more than people think we do. We know when things are over.

So we squeezed.

"It's a living" was a joke in the old days. Now the joke being on you is a way of life.

Hollywood

Dying had become pretty old for Len Turman by the time he turned forty-six. He'd played the voice of a robot, and the robot had died. He'd been the young black dude in a platoon of brave men, and he'd died. He'd played a sword-wielding immortal and felt good that in the film he was supposed to have lived over four thousand years...until an older, evil immortal deceived and decapitated him. He'd had things rammed into him, poured over him, sliced diagonally across him, shot through him, horribly-gone-wrong spliced into him, lemming-ed off a cliff, absorbed, bitten in half, exploded, knifed, poisoned, burned, and even—as the only black man in a film about the French revolution—guillotined. He'd performed every stunt imaginable and acted against a rainbow assortment of special effects screens. He had yet to have onscreen sex, which is why he got into acting in the first damn place, and today was his birthday. Birthdays were tailor-made for deciding when certain shit was about to stop.

Len Turman made calls. He wasn't a bad actor, so he made convincing calls. By the time he was done there were twelve black men of varying ages, incomes and acting abilities parked outside his home. Of the twelve, two were famous enough for paparazzi, and before you knew it Len Turman was in front of the TV cameras looking the world dead in the eye and telling Hollywood:

"We quit.

"No more will we die while lesser actors go on to numerous sequels. No more will we turn our backs on wounded villains or provide chewable ethnic flavor."

"Well," somebody said.

"We are not your surprise twist endings, your tragi-comic sidekicks, or your security officers. We are actors, dammit—"

"Well, well."

"We are men!"

"Full grown."

"We are not going to be the characters everybody knows not to invest too much interest in!"

"Bubba was my best good friend!"

"Oh, no! To quote our great acting brother, we are huge, we are monumental... King Kong ain't got shit on me!"

"Jungle boogie!"

"Effective immediately, if the subplot calls for somebody to die, it's gonna be from somebody a whole lot shades lighter than me."

So a bunch of light-skinned brothers got work. But it wasn't the same, everybody knew it. Movie-goers knew it. The right expectation just wasn't there. The 'Why A Brother Gotta Die?' movement kept growing and growing, until eight months later Len was found buck naked and OD'd between two silicon mounds whose dark carpet most certainly did not match the highlights on her blonde head. Except he'd been married for eighteen years and was more than in love with his wife, he was friends with her.

Word filtered quicker than was likely that Len Turman was a known titty man. Jessica Kitaen's titties were fake, but they were the best fake money could buy. Fox News aired snotty hourly segments on the downfall of the so-called 'Man with a Mission,' and it didn't take long before light-skinned brothers returned to working as lawyers or shifty boyfriends. Darker brothers returned to work too: Hollywood memorialized Len Turman the only way it knew how. Made a bunch of movies about him.

"Let me tell you what's been on m'mind, mate. Devil babies. Little tykes all cold and emotionless gangin' up on nannies and hackin' 'em to bits."

"Everything all right, mate?"

"Been watchin' me own. Got the reverend comin' over tonight."

"That'll do."

"Sooner's better. Sod havin' devil babies about your life."

"How's rev to handle all thirteen? Are you workin' in shifts?"

"Me and the misses'll slip a little sleep in their cocoa."

"Beauty!"

"So when Rev comes 'round 'is biggest problem'll be havin' the bleedin' demons hear 'im over all the snoring."

"There's always a rub."

"Good counsel as always."

"Psshaw! Gives me purpose."

"Right, then."

Thirteen pairs of grubby little eyelids slipped like a lush, flutter flittered a bit, and closed.

"Luvvie, it'll be the devil's time pickin' 'em up. Like dropped flies, they are."

Number nine, whose grip had never been firm to begin with, tumbled from his roost on the family heirloom (a pawn shop chandelier).

"Watch that!"

Father was already diving for the catch. "Don't worry it; I've got 'im." He tossed the boy onto the sofa. Already there were five asleep on it, moptops with nasal passages snoring like banshees. "Damn fine catch that, eh?"

Mother stepped her apron-body over a little one sprawled on the floor, and had to lean close to father to speak as the thumping and tumbling and godawful snores put out more than enough of their own.

"Here's a thought. What with the factories foldin' up I should think a good choice would be to sell the lot off to the American cinema, provided Reverend can't cleanse the devil off their souls."

"The lot? Maybe keep a few?"

"And never sleep a peaceful night again?"

"Point made, Luv."

Religiously hearty poundings pounded the door.

Father hurried to answer.

The gaunt figure of Reverend Slip stood centered in the doorway of the humble dwelling. The little flat square of white below his pointy Adam's apple was a beacon against batwing robes.

"Show me the 'eathens," was all. No greeting, just "Show me the 'eathens," and moved right inside like a line with legs.

"Wait just now," Father tossed, turning after him. "They've been brought up proper. This's just one of them aborigines."

Reverend Slip dropped a heavy duffel for loud effect. "If Satan could hold them at all then they're a far fetch from righteousness. Where's tea, Mother?"

Her hand flew to her mouth.

And as a matter of fact there did issue from the reverend one sharp, audible intake of air. "No tea?" Looking at Father like a man suddenly betrayed he blurted, "Biscuits at least?"

"Well what with the kids I forgot to kettle!" Mother exclaimed, trading worried glances with Father.

"Some things you simply do not forget, Mother," Father said, then offered a placatory smile toward the reverend.

"How am I to function? You invite me into your home—how can I be the savior of your children if you can't even observe the social graces? I know beggars much poorer than you who I can always count on to give with joy to the church!"

"Tea, Mother," Father urged, nodding toward the tiny kitchen. She skittered off, muttering and mumbling at herself as she dug deeply in her apron pockets for little packets of sugar.

"Have you biscuits, then?"

Father swallowed nervously.

"M'God," muttered Reverend Slip. During which (accompanied by a rancid odor that screwed noses up for blocks around) in the kitchen, having just stepped out of a particularly narrow shadow, popped Big Red itself, except it wasn't red and was rather sensitive about racial stereotyping. Rather a short one actually. Unmistakably evil.

Reverend rushed the kitchen hoping ahead of time the stench hadn't come from a mishap with a biscuit substitute. As the reverend's reaction to such an unmistakably evil presence—"What the bloody hell's this?"—was voicing, Father was hoping that feigning ignorance might make the tackily dressed bugger leave off. The devil, to clarify.

"Who're you?"

"Bloody 'ell!" it rasped. "Anybody in the human race not daft? Satan!"

Man can't depend on anything anymore, Father fretted. He rubbed his bulbous nose. "Yes, well, you're—"

"I know I'm late! Lost me head in the U.S. God, America! Bloody piss me off, I don't mind telling you. Now I'm here. Let's have to."

"Now waitaminute," Reverend said. "What's this?"

"Eh?" said Satan.

"A direct confrontation? I'm not here for that!"

"Stop chokin' your scrot. Heard devil babies were about, came to give a look. Curiosity, you know. Vested interests and such. Observation only, Reverend."

"See to it, then!"

"Show some care, Rev," hissed Mother. "Just might piss 'im off."

"Right, where would that leave us?" Father put to him.

"Pretty buggered, I would think," trilled Satan, strolling out to have a look at its alleged progeny.

"These aren't babies! A friggin' rugby team!"

"Some may be a bit big for their age," Mother defended.

"They don't even look like me." It nudged ol' Mother with its elbow. "Eh, Mother?"

"You be havin' tea as well," Father interjected starchily.

"No sugar, Mum, that's the lass." And it patted her doughy rump to send her off. "To business then," Satan said, drawing the two men further into the sitting room.

"I am here strictly to establish paternity," the reverend reminded assertively, adding with a terribly hopeful eye, "Unless you simply want to own up right here?"

"They really don't look a thing like me." It frowned. "No, go to it, Rev."

Father hawed a bit. "What, uh, what if they happen to—"

"Not to worry. I make it a point to always travel with damn fine cigars on me."

By which time even the eyes of dogs and parakeets in the neighborhood welled up. Those in the devil's immediate presence had tried a discreet show of it, but finally Father had to ask, "Whatever 'tis you're givin' off could you tone it down a bit?" There were some annoyances a man shouldn't have to deal with in his own house, by God.

"Do I offend?" It smiled a coquettish, broad, cigar stained smile at Reverend Slip. It puppeted one of the sleeping children, a girl, to open a window as there wasn't a single one open, at which point the atmosphere of the squalid house rushed to flood the entirety of the rest of the world, leaving Father's flat somewhat fresh and comfortably cool. Consequently, a particular breed of monkey that monitors the activities of Satan unanimously decided to forego evolution, ensuring a complete lack of scented toilet paper in the world after the house-apes blew off. Their reasoning: Why give the devil its due? Several parakeets whose owners constantly talked to them committed suicide within moments of the window opening.

Father breathed deeply. He heard the quick aerosol can of country potpourri in the kitchen: Mother hoping the spray would take to this newly freshened air as it was the only freshened air the flat had recently entertained.

"Tea, Father?" Satan smugly inquired.

"Shall we!" Reverend Slip, unsteeled, unsettled, and quite extraordinarily put out about the entire situation, straight-lined to the children. It did not do for the Misses of the house to be spraying potpourri on air freshened by the devil.

He peered closely at the sleeping faces. One particularly showed signs of evil, muttering incoherent phrases and unnatural numerical chants, the middle lad, Reverend surmised from the boy's advanced size. Middle's the best place for corrupting behind and ahead. The reverend indicated with his nose for Father and Satan to give note. "What is this, yes?"

Father coughed and spoke into his hand. "Stocks."

A tick developed beneath the reverend's right cheek. "Again, Father?"

Aghast, Father glanced between Rev and Satan indecisively a moment, sputtered something almost apologetic for destroying what was the Rev's first sure thing, then, gripped with the sudden parental insight and resolve of placing blame where it lay, hurried across and rapped the sleeping boy once across the head to close him off.

And as mum marched primly forward she exhorted chirpily, "Tea?"

Well, the room did brighten a bit, didn't it?

As they drank (without conversation), Satan couldn't help noticing Mother's rather conspicuous way of peering over her cup's rim each time it took a swallow. In a huff, it acknowledged her rudeness.

"Where's yer tongue?" she said directly.

Father and Reverend glanced her way.

"He's got no tongue." Damned if she'd be made to feel untoward in her own home for pointing out someone's improper anomalies. "Had it when he came in."

"Must've swallowed it!" Satan snapped. "Daft ass Brits."

His most manly, world-wearied sigh came from Father, who set his cup in the callused palm of his hand and proclaimed, "We take tea proper in this house when we take it."

"Bloody well came in with it," Mother was saying to Rev, who nodded his support.

"Shall I cough it up?" It hawked a drag, eyeing all. No one responded.

In silence they drank on.

After tea, Satan said, "I'll be off now," and unmistakably meant that there was no reason it should even begin to think those children were its.

"Are you quite certain?" Father asked. "A lot of 'em here. Been off a bit, they have."

"Definitely a good right number, and they're an unpleasant lot. Can I fault them their genes? But realistically, how could they be mine when they're all bloody tranquilized? Don't you think they'd have had enough about them to hack you to bits before you could slip 'em all the mickey?"

Reverend Slip, not one to refute logic, zipped up his duffel sack. "Take example in my utter lack of self-deception in the face of things irrefutable," he said to Father.

"All the best," Satan tipped with a cordial nod.

Reverend ignored it. "Be taking my leave. Father. Mother."

Gone, like a line with legs.

A bit of a scene now. Mum and Dad entertaining Satan--without, recall, biscuits--and thirteen very economically taxing progeny in a little flat on West Buttles. What to do, what to do? ("Stop whizzing!" Reverend shouted trying to dodge all the crying dogs congregated outside this West Buttles home.) "Can you make 'em all politicians then?" Mother asked in an unusual fit of genius.

Satan seemed startled not to have proposed this itself.

Father goggled Mother's way in astonishment.

"The lot?" Satan inquired.

"Well, not all at once, I suppose."

"Sellin' off our children on installment plan?" Father considered this a moment then asked of Satan, "How much soul we talkin', me and the misses to you?"

"No money down, laddie." With an overly large, inhumanly pleased smile that showcased each of its brown teeth, Satan winked. "Politicians I consider an even trade." It took a cigar from its plaid vest pocket and bit the nub off.

Mother smiled inwardly across her slumbering lot, proud, proud. The wafting of country potpourri seemed so much richer now, as though the air recycled and became a step fresher each time, and would confidently keep doing so. Why, soon as this Satan business was over she had a mind to run out and purchase another can.

Father, as only fathers do, slapped then rubbed his stinging thighs to indicate the pleasurable completion of a rather wary situation. He, too, felt a surge of pride knowing without doubt his children would grow up to be respectable, profitable citizens, politicians no less, although, knowing Satan, there'd be some hidden loop and one of them would turn out to be a lawyer, but even that was livable and Father breathed his own short sigh of relief along with an amicable nod of the head, communicating that the boys at the pub would never believe this.

"Believe you me, lad," he responded to the devil, "you're a fair shakes fairer than me lender."

Melba

Psychically linked, Melba participated in her first weapons search a few days before her tenth birthday. The squad torched a tiny encampment after being tipped off to a hidden cache. Seven died: two children, four men, one squad member too close to a hut when the ammunition it held exploded, and a woman, particularly a woman. While she was alive Steak had found the huddled woman in a corner of a thatch hut. He didn't know that Melba's brother was in the doorway watching but not seeing. He didn't know a lot of things. He only knew that he was no longer human with the woman beneath him whose life he forcibly choked; there were acrid smells, the greasy heat of fires, and the release of rage.

She died quickly. Choking was for silence. Steak knew knives. One quick slice.

Melba's brother finally forced the courage to speak.

"Steak," he whispered. "Steak?"

The big man whirled, knife at the ready to end another. It was only James. He put the knife away haltingly, still wet with bits of meat.

"What'd you see, boy?" Steak glowered at him. His eyes caught the dance of the fires.

"Nothin' at all, Steak." Her brother held his palms up. "Not a damned thing."

"You damn well saw nothin'!" Then he advanced. Steak was a thick piece of meat with muscles in his lips. He grabbed James by the collar and hauled him like cloth away from the door. The boy glimpsed the small woman's folded body over Steak's shoulder before being yanked again.

"C'mon, Steak! Steak!"

"Just James. James don't see nothin'." Steak released him. "James'glasses is broke." He choked on air then laughed.

"Yeah. My glasses is broke, and I can't see nothin'. C'mon, Steak, let's go. Hell away from here, awright?"

"Blind with your goddamn glasses broke, fool. Not here. Fix that shit, 'cause I plan on goin' insane." He did so during one of the long nights. Ran screaming and firing into the black jungle. Charlie was the jungle. Charlie'd eat him alive, the entire company knew it, so they stayed low, stayed quiet, and were ashamed of the way their fingers clawed deep into the moist ground and the grass itched their faces. Melba believed she'd die that night. Her brother the same. She cried, wondering if he knew what he was doing to her. She crept out of bed, down the hall, and out the front door to watch the night and stars which eased her mind.

Nam gave himself to her that night. The big, lazy cat watched her sitting on her steps and decided to curl up beside her for the night. Didn't really acknowledge her presence at all. It rudely went to sleep. Melba scooped it up and carried it back to her room.

The next day Melba fell in love. With me. I can't help but smile. She's sedated now.

We met in Matthew Memorial Park. I was playing with friends: Batman and Robin team up with Captain Kirk and Mr. Spock against the Joker and Penguin plus henchmen. I was the Captain. Two henchmen were trying to capture me to give to the Penguin. Being Kirk, I had to win, which I did, but gave a henchman a bloody nose by mistake. His crying broke up the game. We stood in the sun telling him to shut up while assuring him he was all right. At Spock's urging I managed an apology. That's when Batman tapped me and told me "some girl behind a tree" wanted to talk to me.

"What're you playing?" she asked, then dodged her eyes from mine.

"Nothin'."

"He said you're the Captain. What's your real name?"

I shrugged. "That's what everybody calls me. What's yours?"

"Melba." She produced something from behind the folds of her dress. "And this is Nam."

"Weird name for a cat. Why'd you name it that?"

She didn't answer.

"What'd you want?" I asked.

She blushed. "Dunno." She dropped Nam to play with her auburn hair. She knelt to sit at the tree's base. I mumbled about her getting her dress dirty, wondering whether I should sit beside her already. She told me the dress was just for show. We talked for a good while.

June 24, 1968. Melba screamed herself awake. Her brother's moans rattled within her. He was in a cage speaking to dead bodies. The cage was suspended half in the river inside a clump of sickly-green moss. He had convinced himself there were leeches. Gunfire sounded. Somewhere. It'd be night soon. He was trying to stay awake, holding to the cage to keep from sliding beneath the water, murmuring to himself that it was so cold, so cold, and I can't see nothin' at all. Can't see nothin' at night. Glasses...broke. I wanna come home, Mama. Steak, you crazy coward bastard, you hear that!? Can't see a damn thing and I wanna go home...

A single heaved sigh sent him downward. The arms gradually loosened around the cage's cane bars. The brine sucked him lower. Sleep pounded him. Moonlight glinted off the cheap ring they hadn't bothered removing from his swollen finger. That attracted it. A cheap, silly ring Melba had given him millennia ago.

His left arm dropped into the muck. Something made his eyes snap open just as the rat's teeth clamped down. He watched his blood add to the engorged waters of this hellish land. He snatched the rat's tail, then it's belly, clawing and squeezing till it released. He flung it against the bars. It flopped into the water and tried to swim away. Broken, it managed only a few sickly ripples. He seized its neck and held it under. Its head crushed long before it had a chance to drown.

Nobody in the cage stirred.

Melba kicked at her sheets, causing Nam to poke its head up and mew for silence. Then she started screaming. Nam rose and left just as her parents entered the room, giving them a brief glance of innocence before sliding out the door.

The next morning: "Do you feel like going to school?"

Her brother was working on an escape plan and didn't need to be bothered. She snapped, "No!" Her parents had already taken her to a therapist, pre-plugging their ears against any word of anything wrong.

Her mother frowned. Punishment had proven useless. Fights at friends' houses and muttering about "gooks" continued. "Go back to bed," she said. "I'll check on you later." Everyone had taken James' draft hard, but not hard enough for this.

'Sorry, Ma,' thought Melba. 'But James needs to concentrate. There's gooks everywhere.'

On a nice day, the kind picnics are made for, I walked by her house on the way to school. When I didn't see her I figured she'd already gone so I took a shortcut through the park.

She was sitting by our tree, looking intently at the ground.

I tried to sneak up on her. A twig snapped. She whirled like a soldier, a small stick in her hand.

"Whutchu doin'?" I asked. "Aren't you going to school?"

"Hell're you doin' creepin' on me? I mighta blew your ass off," she muttered.

Wondering if I'd heard correctly, in complete shock, I asked again, "You goin' to school?"

She smiled the smile of a pixie. "Nope."

Nam ambled over to sit and stare at me.

"Does that cat ever leave you alone?"

She had gone back to watching the grass. "Don't bother me," she said distractedly.

Was she referring to the cat or me? I sat beside her.

She glanced at me—"You'll be late," then brightened when I shrugged and said I wasn't going.

"Good. We can play here all day and have a picnic and—"

"What were you doing?"

She pushed hair away from her eyes. "When?"

"Lookin' at the grass."

She laughed. "Look down there." She pointed out a patch with her stick.

Bending, I saw that the grass was alive with ants. Not very many, they marched single file with tiny bits of leaf or worm in their mandibles. Looking closer I saw a larger ant on its back, its abdomen curled to its head. One of the smaller ants pushed at it, then, seeing it wasn't up to the task, enlisted the aid of its brothers to turn it on its side. They proceeded to tear bits of the dead ant off, taking the legs and antennae, leaving the rest for others. They scurried back to their group, walking clumsily with their relatively large forage.

I'd seen the sight many times and didn't find any special significance in this one. I looked to Melba, whose fascination was also wearing off.

"You should've seen it when they first started. The little brown ones were carrying that stuff and the black one came and they started fighting and first the big one was winning, then the little ones ganged up and killed him. That's how you're supposed to do it. He died easy too. And they tore him up."

Her voice went progressively lower, until she was speaking in a throaty whisper.

"That's what you do to gooks. And gook women. You cut their throats and...and...and you kill the bastard before he kills you,'" she said so low I barely heard it. She got to her feet.

The air felt funny. I had to say something. "Want to have a picnic?"

Her mask softened. She brushed dirt off her jeans. "A picnic? A picnic! Yeah! If you want. And we can go swimming—no, not swimming, but a picnic. With a basket and blanket and stuff."

We went in search of picnic goods, with Nam right beside us.

I waited behind a tree while she got the blanket and basket from her house.

She told her mother she was going on a picnic. Her mother looked out the kitchen window. "Is that him hiding behind the tree?"

When Melba laughed her mother nearly cried.

"Go on then."

Melba bounced out the door.

I stepped out. "Your mother never knew I was there!"

"Nope."

And the day was ours until Nam returned after a long hunt and dropped a mouse at our feet, preening himself before dinner. Melba threw the basket at the cat.

"Godammit, cat! Get the hell out of here!"

Nam, ruffled momentarily, composed himself and trotted away.

I didn't say anything.

Melba suddenly ran from our tree to another. I followed. When I caught up she turned to me, crying.

"God damn Charlie. Damn Nam. Damn Vietnam! I hate them! James. I hate him! Crying to his little sister for help. No more!" She couldn't control the tears.

James?

I wanted to run away but my arm went around her shoulders.

James?

"Melba?" Oh God, what? "Um..." (Christ!) "Melba, what's wrong?" It wasn't enough wondering what would Kirk do. If she didn't stop soon I'd be crying too. "Melba, I can help."

She fought to calm herself.

"I can help. Stop crying."

"Make James stop. If it's so bad why doesn't he just come home?"

I scoured my mind for a James. Only James I knew was James T. Kirk.

"Who's James?"

"My brother." She dabbed at her eyes with a corner of her shirt. They'd become red and puffy.

"Didn't know you had a brother."

She was down to sniffles.

"Where is he?"

"In Nam. Vietnam."

I searched again. Vietnam? Oh yeah. The war.

"He'll be coming back though," I said. "Doesn't he send you letters and stuff?"

She almost smiled. "Mostly stuff." She dabbed her eyes again. "He's already here. He sits in my room."

We sat. This would be our new tree.

She began to pull up blades of grass.

"Andy, can you keep a good secret, one you don't ever think about?"

"How can you not—" Then: "I can keep a secret."

"Andy, Captain..."

"Andy."

"Andy. Listen. Don't ask or anything. Just listen. Don't even look at me while I'm talking. Not like headshrink Morrisey."

"Dr. Morrisey? My mom works for him. She used to talk about a girl who beat him up. I met him a few times."

Melba was looking dead at me.

"That was me. Now shut up."

Wind whipped in through a half-opened windshield, early spring five years ago, Clement Road, a grey car driving flat out and wild down a little-traveled stretch with a dead tree across the road around the next bend. James saw it too slowly and nearly exploded in fear. She was home in bed when his foot rammed the brake.

They hit the tree. During her nap, her head throbbed suddenly. The tree superimposed her dreams; she saw it in the road through the glass and knew she was going too fast to stop. Turning her head, there was Byron Saunder pointing, then James slammed the brake and the old ironhorse reared back. She jumped awake with a splitting headache an hour before James' sheepish call came. No serious damage beyond egos, bruises and wet pants, but she never told anyone, not even him, where she had been. She's never told anyone at all but me.

Fear is the key.

During the years other episodes followed.

James was sent to Vietnam for three years. Three in the pit. Three years he escaped its horrors by sending them off. Like a garbage disposal: garbage in, flick the switch, and Melba had to deal with it. Her first taste was Steak shooting madly at a tree. James tried to calm him, causing Steak to turn on him, his gun level with her brother's face.

James hid, leaving Melba to stand Steak down.

He lowered the gun and stalked off.

She once told me that sometimes she felt sorry for Steak. He had to keep his stuff himself.

He should've had a little sister.

She would be awakened at night, or sometimes fight in daytime, by James. I hated James. James with his stupid war. James with his stupid mind. They gave him a medal when he came back. Melba didn't get one, but she didn't care. James was back. I hate James.

My eyes opened. "Can I talk?"

She nodded.

"Do you feel things?"

"Like what?"

"Like pain."

"I don't know. It hurts sometimes. He's scared a lot. That's worse."

I nodded. "What are you going to do?"

"Go crazy."

"Don't—"

"I mean it. Andy, I go around talking about gooks and fighting, and I see, I hear things, at night."

I sighed a half-hearted wish that she was making this up.

"You said you'd help."

"I will. All the time."

We stayed by the tree, not speaking but thinking a lot. For once, Nam left us alone. We stayed till first dark, which meant trouble. It didn't matter. She wanted to listen to the stars. Since I didn't know their language she translated, and every story was peaceful.

It cooled quickly. We gathered our things. I wouldn't let her carry anything and she kissed me on the cheek. We headed home. I looked for Nam. There he was, creeping at a distance.

June 30, 1968: Bastard gooks shoulda known couldn't keep us down. But we lost Jules, only six now. But that's all right. We can do it. Gotta do it. Dammit, what is it? Hand's killing me. Medic got it before they had to cut it off. Pumped me fulla shots. Hurts like hell. Those shots I heard—Ours! Hell yeah! Blew livin' life outta Charlie. Yeah. Got us outta that damn cage. Yes, Lord, but they got Jules. Fucker wasn't dead, and when Jules came out, fucker fired on him. Just like that. I snatched a sub and fried him. Gooks die easy. Robert's getting sent home. The green got him. That's five. Ok. We'll rest, get some more weapons, and act like we don't know a goddamned thing about mercy.

Clouds floated quickly past. Now it was July 9, 1968, and I was on the ground with head tilted back, not admiring the sky or lost in imagination but trying to keep blood from trickling out my nose. I was glad she'd run off. I was angry enough to have hit her back if she'd stayed.

Tired of her being so damn crazy.

Right after she left, Spock abandoned the group he'd been playing with and sat by me.

"What'd you do?"

"I didn't do nothin'." The taste of blood made me queasy. "I need some tissue."

Spock worked hard at a grass stain on the toe of his new sneakers. He gave up on the stain. "Don't have any." He pushed up and left.

Melba was on her way back.

I saw that she had something. She came to me and cheerfully plopped to her knees, thrusting a rectangle in front of my eyes.

It was a picture.

"It's too close," I said.

She moved it back instead of letting me hold it myself.

"Who's he?" I asked.

She knew I knew but answered anyway. "That's my brother. That's James."

"I don't want to see him." Ever since she'd told me about him and Vietnam I tried to pretend he didn't exist.

Melba laid the photograph on the grass, a hurt expression on her face. She watched me steadily with her hard-edged eyes before raising the corner of her mouth in a tiny, humorless smile. She said, "My brother is a warrior. See—" she pointed at the picture, blades of grass sticking out all around it—"that's him, and this is Vietnam." She ran fingers through the grass.

"This isn't Vietnam."

"You'll never see it for real so shut up."

I held my finger to my nose a second to make certain the bleeding had stopped. I sniffed for effect.

She picked the photo up and marched it through the grass. "James is gonna come home soon," she said offhand.

"How do you know?"

"They'll give him medals and awards."

"For what?"

"He's fighting for his country," she said gravely.

"That's something you heard on TV or your father."

"My father never says anything important."

"What about your mother?" Seconds passed. I thought she hadn't heard me. She was staring off at everything, her eyes nearly glassy, her body perfectly still.

"Melba?" I kept watching her eyes. She hadn't blinked. Then she choked back a sob, but it wasn't coming from her. I glanced around, hoping some adult would come knowing what to do. "Melba? Come on, come back."

"They're going to kill him. He knows it. Charlie doesn't stop. If they don't get him over there they're going to follow him here. He knows. There's nothing he can do."

Nobody was coming.

"He's hiding...but he's watching." Her breathing was a series of frightened shallow pants.

"Stop it!" I grabbed and shook her.

She blinked but her eyes weren't there. "I'm fine, Andy," she whispered. "Charlie doesn't hunt me over here. I check under my bed every night and every morning, and I'm all right." She trembled in my grip, then winced and tore away from me. She threw herself flat and threw an arm over her head, the other hand clawing at the grass. "If you run you die. Stay down!"

I knew kids had stopped to see what was going on, but I was crying and they wouldn't come toward me. Even the adults, a few of them had stopped, but no one moved.

Her head shot up then. Out of the corner of my eye I saw the familiar shape of Nam coming toward us. The cat padded warily within distance, its hackles raised. It stopped a few feet from her, uncertain whether or not to run away.

Melba grabbed the cat in a flash. It hissed wildly as it struggled. She tightened her grip on its neck and hugged an arm around its body. Then she ran.

I bolted after her but she was too fast.

She ran inside her house, leaving me outside. She'd gone in through the backyard. I hopped the fence and stopped.

A motion at an upstairs window caught my eye. I looked up to see the window being slowly raised.

"Melba, stop!"

Through a vacuum came the sounds of others approaching, and when I looked it was her mother and father running out of a neighbor's across the street. Returning my attention to the window, I dumbly watched as she held her arm outward, Nam dangling and clawing at the air. Bloody scratches along her arm formed a red grid of jagged lines.

Her mouth was working. She was saying over and over, softly but audibly for me: "Nam won't die. Cats always land on their feet. Nam won't die."

She flung the cat down.

It hit the dry ground right in front of me, in a puff of dust, not three feet away.

My gaze went from the dead cat to the little girl standing at the window above me. She was crying. Her eyes met mine.

Her father ran into the house, followed a moment later by her mother, who had stopped beside me a second to make sure I wasn't injured. I felt very small left alone in the dirt of their backyard with two inquisitive flies already lighting on the cat's body.

"Andy."

Heavier tears welled up in my eyes. They made my bottom lip quiver.

"Andy...I miss James."

I walked slowly to the tree in their backyard, where I hid myself against it, my back pressed so hard against the bark it hurt. I sat on the side away from the window, away from the small body in the dirt, and tried not to hear as Melba called down to me:

"James is home, Andy."

I am African-American. America was not in the business of importing slaves. They brought in ninjas, scores of ninjas. And, myself being one of them, we are still invisible to this day. I recall when I was Japanese. This country has seen the deaths of beautiful things.

I don't know the Japanese word for sadness.

No one would believe he was crying for a wave as he stood inches from the water's edge. All that way and it had not even reached to moisten his toes.

He had stared outward while it approached. He tried his best to follow that one wave—being six and not knowing about physics—wishing that people would get out of the water and out of its way. His head tilted downward and downward the closer it came, until the dimpled chin almost touched his chest. It was while he stood that way that his sisters noticed him and his tears.

Tamiro and Miyashi watched him a moment for time to decide something was wrong, and also to see which would have responsibility for him. Miyashi pushed off in the shallow water.

"What's wrong with you?" Miyashi asked in a flat but concerned fashion.

He loved his sisters, nearly worshipped Miyashi, who was fourteen, but did not want his answer to be dismissed by them as silly.

"Nothing," he said without looking at either one. The streaks were still on his face, but he had not really noticed his own tears until one had fallen from its hold on his left cheek to clear off a small space on his left foot.

A bright red beach ball flew by them and into the shallows. A skinny girl with wet straw hair ran after it. A troop of three twenty-one year olds, a black with intricate braids, a deeply tanned white wearing a T-shirt with many large holes cut in it, and their oldest sister, Daemora, chased her.

He watched through the space between Miyashi and Tamiro's bodies as the blond girl splashed into the water. Just as she grabbed the ball she was tackled.

With much whooping and screeching the four bodies toppled into the water, arms and legs everywhere. They were close enough to the children for droplets of their splashing and thrashing to strike upon the backs of Tamiro and Miyashi.

"What are you crying for then?"

He focused on the ocean. His eldest sister and her friends remained fuzzy in the foreground. Someone from over the horizon had sent the wave on its way, he thought, and saw different pictures of lonely children on a beach's edge. Someone had tried to touch him, must have wanted to very badly to have undertaken such a solitary journey for so long, night and day across all that water. Somehow that made him feel guilty and responsible.

"I'm not," he said. On his face the streaks had dried into the pores of his pale skin. He was a spindly child with dry charcoal hair that hung neatly from his round head.

"You want to go home?" Tamiro asked.

He shook his head.

"Then go play instead of standing by yourself. You haven't even been swimming all the time we've been here."

"I don't know these people," he said and motioned slightly to specify which people. Yards down the beach a group of four children were smashing a sand castle, heaping buckets of water atop its towers and against its walls. As he watched, one of them looked his way, then ran for more water.

"Yugi," Miyashi said, "you can play with us."

Yugi answered in a mumble. "I don't feel like playing." He brought his focus back to the immediate surroundings. He looked at Miyashi. "Will you be like Daemora when you get bigger?"

"Daemora can't always pay attention to you," Miyashi said. "She's like mother and father now. You understand?"

"He'll have both of us standing here like him," Tamiro complained, irritated and impatient. There was nothing really wrong. She wanted to have fun.

"You go ahead," Miyashi told her.

"Should I get Daemora?"

Miyashi shook her head no. "I'll be along too."

Yugi watched Tamiro dash back into the water. She swam less energetically, and stopped at a spot where there were no people to simply float. The back of her head was to them as she stared outward, past the safety netting and its bobbing orange markers, straight out to the horizon that underlined the blue sky and its sparse clouds.

"Why are you acting like this, Yugi? You stand by yourself and say that you're lonely." Miyashi fixed him with her stare, making him look into her face.

Daemora and her friends were running along the surf. The white with the tattered shirt now had the ball and was loud as he raced just a few steps ahead of his pursuers.

"It's my fault it died," Yugi said. He could no longer keep eye contact with his beloved sister.

"Watch what you say! If I hear that again you'll be in trouble!"

Yugi's head snapped up at her tone.

"What?"

"Be quiet. If you don't want to play, then don't. Go lie on the blanket and keep our things. We'll be leaving soon anyway; Daemora has to cook and get ready for tomorrow."

"When are we leaving?"

"I don't know. Soon. Go ask Daemora."

"She's too far down."

"They're chasing her back," Miyashi said looking in the direction of the fast approaching four. Daemora clutched the big beach ball tightly to her chest, swinging it with her torso left and right as she ran. She caught Yugi's eye and winked at him as she sped by.

Miyashi shouted a playful "Hey!" at all the muck kicked under their big feet.

Miyashi waited to get Daemora's attention till after her sister got tackled and they were attempting to extricate themselves. She waved while shouting, "Daemora!"

"Wait a minute!" Daemora shouted back. She was waist deep in the water and trying to keep her footing. A large wave knocked against her back and flowed around her. She held her arms out horizontally, placing a hand on the blond girl's shoulder to steady herself.

She waded through the water, mostly long legs and hair in a purple bathing suit. Yugi watched the funny sway of her hips and felt the tiny traces of a grin somewhere between walls. She reminded him of the ladies on TV commercials.

She reached the two children. Still smiling, she asked, "What is it?"

"When are we leaving?" Miyashi asked.

Daemora's eyes widened. "You're not ready to go, are you?"

"I was just wondering," Miyashi said.

Daemora looked down at her baby brother. Her brow creased. She returned her attention to Miyashi. Sighing, she said, "In a few minutes. I keep thinking today's Saturday. I've got you and me to get ready for tomorrow."

"Daemora, can I go somewhere?" Yugi asked.

"Depends," she answered and grinned at him. "Where to?"

"How far is it from here to where the waves come from?"

"The ocean? If you're going sailing, I don't know. That's thousands of miles for one little boy."

"I'll do it," he said.

Miyashi pointed out to Tamiro. "Should I tell Tamiro to come in?"

"If you want. But it'll be about fifteen minutes before we start packing. I owe Susan a few hits."

Her friends were standing in the water waiting for her.

"Set?" she asked the two children.

Miyashi nodded.

"Ok. Fifteen minutes, right?"

"Right," Miyashi said to her sister's back. Daemora had turned and was running through the water to her friends.

Miyashi wondered what she should do for the remaining fifteen minutes. She could go back and swim and play water tag with Tamiro—if she still wanted to play—or stay standing with Yugi while everyone else had fun. But she didn't feel like staying with Yugi. He was young, but that was no excuse; it had been nearly four months. In her mind she *hmmphed!* His fault!

She became aware of him staring at her.

"What now?"

Yugi fidgeted. He did not want Miyashi mad at him. "How much is fifteen minutes?"

"Why?"

"Nothing. I just want to know."

"It's not a lot of time."

"How much?"

Near exasperation she exhaled sharply and said, "Look. See the orange markers? It's as much as it would take you to swim out there."

He saw the distance. He'd never done it before. His parents had never let him, and now Daemora would not. He tugged the hem of Miyashi's swimsuit to stop her before she left him.

"Don't do that." She waited with folded arms for him to ask his question.

"Are you going back with Tamiro now?" he asked.

She nodded. She turned to go then turned back to him. "I guess I don't have to tell you not to go anywhere since you've been happy standing in this spot, but don't go anywhere. If you're bored, stay on the blanket where Mrs. Omata can see you and play in the sand. I'll be watching you too," she said, "so stay where I can see you."

She ran off as Daemora had, but her splash wasn't as big. Yugi remained at the surf's edge in his same footprints and watched her swim out to Tamiro, who saw her coming and dove beneath the water in hide and seek.

Daemora and her loud friends were again thrashing like hooked fish.

And the children with the mud castle were piling dry sand atop the wet mess they'd made.

As the moments passed, Yugi watched and felt anger. He looked down at his toes, at the spot that had made him feel as though everything was his fault, then lifted his tiny feet out of their small footprints in the sucking sand and walked quickly along the beach's edge. At times the splash and surf of incoming waves reached to wash or cool his sand-warmed feet. He walked in the direction that took him away from where Daemora, Miyashi and Tamiro could see him, and tried to weave in and out among the other bathers so that Mrs. Omata would not notice and call out.

No one stopped him. He had covered nearly thirty yards before he stopped to look at the space between where he was and where he'd been. Daemora and her friends, and Miyashi and Tamiro who were farther down than they, looked small and smaller. None of them had noticed that he was gone.

He had come to a relatively clear section of the beach. The people there napped on the beach sunning. He waded into the water until it reached to lap at his knobby knees. He held his arms out before him and launched himself with a push against the yielding sand bed into the ocean, holding his head high above the water and making a sour face at its shocking coolness. He swam as quickly as his arms and legs would move him, as fast as his neck could turn to let him inhale and exhale. Even then, though to himself he was moving quickly, it took him a minute past the time Miyashi had given, but his mind was not on that.

Panting, he reached one of the bobbing orange markers, as bright as the orange trunks he wore. His eyes widened in fear at how near he was to being *out there*. He would only have to slip over the netting. He allowed his body to rotate, floating like the marker with the motions of the waves. Daemora, Miyashi and Tamiro were far away, little like him. When his body faced ocean line again he began to thrash about. His arms moved like frantic wings atop the water that splashed back into his face. His eyes were squints, and lids blinked like hummingbirds to keep the droplets from entering them. Beneath the water his legs fought to keep him afloat. His heart beat painfully. He had never had so much water between him and the wet sands that his toes stretched for. His head bobbed beneath the water. For a second he felt swallowed. His legs kicked for the surface. He met air, gasping and choking. His silent thrashings grew wilder and more frantic. He had no idea which direction he faced. He would not open his eyes. In his small mind he desperately wished for gills, but the arms had to keep moving. They hurt. His legs felt like weights to drag him under, and the water had thickened to honey.

Yugi felt vibrations, strong, not his own, and heard the noise of quick, rhythmic splashing. He opened his eyes. He was facing the beach, facing Daemora at the head of a group all coming toward him. She swam right into the waves he was making. They touched the lifeguard behind her. Yugi felt Daemora's arms encircle him, and felt himself pulled tightly to her. The lifeguard came alongside them.

The boy was taken back to the shore. Daemora dropped to her knees in the sand, still clutching him tightly. There was a crowd of people all around them, many looking on with concern, some voicing relief. He picked out those of Tamiro and Miyashi.

Daemora held him at arm's length to look at him.

"What were you doing? Yugi! Do you know you could've drowned? What made you do that? What were you trying to do?"

Her grip on his shoulders had tightened slightly. As she looked into his eyes, and he looked fearfully into her own, his eyes misted, then watered, and he began to cry. His lips trembled and a whimper rose up from his heart. Water ran down from his hair and blended with the slow tears streaking his chin. He tried to mutter something but nothing came out. Daemora gathered him back into her arms and stood. She carried him up the beach. People trailed behind. She carried him away from the water. His vision bobbed with her steps. Up and down the ocean moved, with the waves still coming. Through his red eyes Yugi peered over his sister's shoulder, searching the ocean for his waves. He wondered if anyone would know that he'd made them and sent them out. He was small but he was strong, and he was sure he would be able to touch someone at the end of his journey across the ocean.

"Are you now or have you ever been a life form?"

A brief pause separated the response from the question. "No, sir, I'm from the States."

Niimu hated when they died as comedians.

A checkmark was made in the ether, then, without so much as an additional thought, Niimu said, "Down the hall, first door. Next."

The sign on the door read: PULVERIZING. IDENTIFY YOURSELF IN THE SCHEME OF THINGS.

Another brief pause. "Human?"

The door split itself into three horizontal panels, and the lowest section slid open. A drab voice intoned, "Slide under."

Awkward. And then there was no one, or thing, or *any*thing inside. "Hello?"

From uniform non-illumination, a spot of light imploded as the checkmaker appeared. "How do you want to return?" it asked unceremoniously. "Or do you prefer random draw?"

Still rubbing eyes. Very awkward. "Huh?"

"Sign said pulverizing, right?"

Nodding. Yes, it had.

"Souls for pulverizing back into raw material. Can't send you back with your memories intact, eh? Create a world of trouble doing that."

"Just came from a world of trouble. I'd prefer something different. But I think there's been a mistake, see?"

The amorphous checkmaker covered its middle mouth with the back of a bulbous appendage so the human wouldn't see it grind its teeth. Then, to the waiting soul, it said: "Explain."

"What happened to heaven?"

"Let's avoid getting so overwhelmed by wonder that we start looking for gods, shall we?" The bottom panel swished open. On its belly, another soul wiggled in. This one was quite naked and quite female.

"Stay by the door," Niimu told her. To the first soul, it said, "There's only supposed to be one to this room at a time. You're backing us up."

"He's kinda cute," the fe-soul piped.

Niimu ignored her. It took the he-soul by the hand, and pulled further into abstract nothing-ness.

"Weren't paying full attention at your processing, were you?"

A glance back at the fe-soul, then, to the weary closing of Niimu's third eye, "She was behind me in line. You might say my mind was occupied."

Niimu shared a thought along the entire continuum of Niimu to send no more through, and to expect no output from pulverizing. Although there was no outward indication, a bubble of time formed around Niimu and the soul.

"This is a reincarnation processing station. Or should I say, *the* reincarnation processing station."

"Right. Aware that I'm dead."

"Good. As for heaven, it isn't part of your, well, *deal*. Not for you, I should say. You're here to be returned to a specific moment in the nowhen. Standard procedure allows for personal choice as to form, but undue delay in decision-making imposes upon me the function of arbiter. You'll be deposited, and accumulate enough functional experiences to warrant being eventually returned here for re-use. A recycling process, and fairly efficient, as long as no one holds up the line. There's only so much diversity one can work into the universe. Imagination is vast, but it's not infinite."

"Shouldn't there be some kind of library period? Give me time to do a little research? I mean, there's so much I don't know, and so many I've never heard of, with all the people and things. Animal species that haven't been found yet, when I came from."

"You can't return as something you don't know about. It's an arguably valid take, but unworkable. Don't stress over the details. Whatever you don't return as this time, you'll eventually get around to. Nothing is lost."

"What about extinction? That seems like a loss."

"Ah!" Niimu opened another mouth that had, until then, remained closed. "Linearity. No, the time of death is insignificant. You can be returned anywhen, anything, any situation. Reality is pretty flexible. Must say, you've never given this much trouble before."

"Me?"

"Not specifically."

"This is all quite fantastic."

"Thank you," responded Niimu. "Now, eternity is not to be delayed forever. As who or what do you wish to return? It takes but a thought, and you needn't fret over tiny specifics. Further processing will see to those."

The he-soul grinned, slyly. "And if I chose you?"

Middle mouth stretched into a wide smile. Not pretty. "Niimu is *quite* fixed in the loop of things."

The bubble negated, and time flowed. The fe-soul was still by the door.

"Are you prepared to proceed?" Niimu queried. Polite.

The he-soul nodded. Instantly Niimu and the fe-soul blinked away, although the he-soul wondered for a moment whether it was he who had gone away, instead of them. But then, immersed in the concept of *Pulverizing*, he became tightly packed, dense, fell crushingly in upon himself until no more empty space could be displaced, and at the moment of critical mass, fell in and through himself and outward again, not in cataclysmic debris, but spreading rather like a gentle rain, slow and peaceful. Finally, stretched almost too thin to recognize himself as anything real, his last thought spilled upon the æther: *A billion lifetimes to choose, and never anything on TV...*

＊ ＊ ＊

"We all want to be the hero," Sergeant Hannspree said, looking each of them in the eye, close enough they smelled his lunch. Without warning he punched Glynnis Dobbins in the stomach so hard Dobbins spit and doubled over. The line almost broke ranks.

"Do you feel like a hero?"

Dobbins coughed and straightened slowly, eyes watery. "Sir, yes, sir."

"Speak so we can hear you."

"Sir, yes, sir!"

"Why is that?"

"Because I am still standing, sir!"

"Yeah, you keep thinking that. When we drop planet I expect cowards out of each and every one of you. A coward will kill anything that moves. Do you understand me?"

"Sir, yes, sir!"

But when they dropped planet for a colonization mission, Dobbins had no idea what to do when a man surrendered. The guns stopped and an indigo man jumped out with webbed hands beating his chest like he couldn't catch hold of it. The man screamed something because guns were pointed at him, and two of the platoon shot him. Two more like the victim jumped from hiding, arms raised toward some high god, crying and swallowing and beating their chests with the flats of their hands.

Dobbins thought they were communicating, clearly, suddenly, and insistently, the fact that although they were trying to kill the soldiers, and trying very hard—because the soldiers were killing them too, very hard—the task was not as important as they thought. Time out.

Indigo bodies, bits and whole, lay scattered over uneven ground.

"Mr. Dobbins is going to kill you, do you understand that?" said Hannspree.

Dobbins swallowed. "Sir?"

"We did not come out here to invite a bunch of blue 'phibians home," Hannspree said quietly. "We did not come out here because we want to be here. And we are not going to leave here without accomplishing what we came to do. Are we in agreement, Dobbins?"

"I'm not going to kill them, sir."

"Yes, you are." Cold.

The platoon edged back.

"These blue, webbed *terrorists*," said Hannspree, "are taking your role. They're standing, Dobbins. Heroes. Are there any other heroes on this planet?"

Every other soldier gripped a weapon, and waited.

"So now I need to know who you are, Mr. Dobbins. Hero or coward?" Hannspree drew a sidearm.

Dobbins had never seen a barrel between his eyes before. He didn't like it.

One of the female medics muttered something religious. The two blue captives breathed so hard that Dobbins wondered whether his own breath had stopped. A single soldier started to lower his weapon, but Hannspree spoke the man's name and it lifted again.

Hanspree whipped the gun to the left, and fired.

The blue man on the left tottered a step. His arms flailed before he went down, and Dobbins thought he looked like a wrecked kite.

The Sergeant's eyes focused on the dying man, as the webbed hand clutched sand. A beat fell against the shore, and then a weak spasm that might have been another strike upon the chest, if it had landed. A dorsal kept the almost-corpse suspended.

And then the Sergeant crumpled.

The entire planet knew Hannspree had lost it.

"You can spin the barrel any way you like," he said, "but some people will never be anything but a name on a bullet. Why are we here, Dobbins? Does this look real to you?"

The platoon edged back a little more. Dobbins edged back with them, and stepped on a finger that had been blown off one of the dead. He jumped toward Hannspree.

The entire platoon knew that wasn't a smart thing to do.

"Oh, son of a mother—!" he swore, as momentum carried him back to the processing station and the Niimu quickly whisked him away.

* * *

The next life he spent all his time destroying relationships without knowing precisely how or why.

* * *

A brief life went into waving cilia, gathering nutrients, and eating smaller organisms.

* * *

Another, she ignored the warnings of her mates and steered their Greenpeace RIB toward a whale calf. A larger whale capsized their boat and all hands drowned. It was shown on the news.

* * *

Yet another time, he was a large whale. He capsized a boat.

* * *

Once, he was blue. That time he got shot in the chest and died clutching a fistful of sand.

* * *

There was once he got to be a superhero.

* * *

Although most souls were beautiful and ethereal and couldn't be destroyed, there were some that were just annoyingly slow learners. How a soul could be a sorceress in one life, yet wind up face down in the muck with a back full of arrows, was as patently absurd as finding itself a theoretical physicist with a degenerative motor neurone disease in the next.

Not that the he-soul ever wound up a theoretical physicist. Theoretical physicists were seldom "slow learners."

* * *

Absurdities, nevertheless, were introduced from time to time. When strange appendages extruded from the sides of his computer, those appendages sprouting more in turn, Ernest recognized the absurdity at once.

They wove themselves into a wall, and more, until he was comfortably encased. Consoles grew out of the walls, lit themselves, and began to flash. From the metallic deck— formerly the laminate floor of his home office—an assortment of chairs sprouted, and from the chairs people, and from the people uniforms and insignia to indicate their relative position and presumptive reason for being positioned in front of a console. A split-level screen grew astern, and a single-level grew ahead. Ernest turned, and upon the lower section of the split screen he saw his living room as it was demolished by the growing technology; the top section showed what he could only assume was intended as the floor plan for some fantastic hotel, with looped corridors that threaded their way through a maze of subdivided rooms, and circled upon themselves in unfathomably chaotic fashion. He faced forward and saw upon the main screen a starfield placed beside a simplified, underscaled planetary system schematic and columns of numeric data. Lights started to blink in front of him, and he stared at the unfamiliar manifestation as text scrolled across the big screen.

Ship's complete, Darvin. ETA rendezvous with P.T.V. Aerie: thirteen minutes. Crew signals ready. End of message, Darvin.

Darvin?

A smaller screen grew atop his monitor, snapped itself loose, and clattered to the console. Ernest read the new message that appeared on it.

Excellent, Darvin. Shuttle ready for lift. Please issue appropriate orders to crew.

"My name isn't Darvin," he replied.

Questioning destiny? Don't be difficult. Please issue appropriate orders to crew.

"Right... OK. Crew? I guess I'll start issuing appropriate orders now." He'd eaten oatmeal cookies and root beer for breakfast. A sugar imbalance might explain the hallucinations.

"Uh, hot jets. Load the torpedoes. Let's go."

Inappropriate, Darvin. Lilac's calling. This is not your time to waste.

Orders as follows: Navigator, scan course for clearance; Helm, initiate drive, point zero-one-five, increase by point zero-zero-five outer boundary; Communications, open for Aerie, leave open; All systems converge. Lift. Do it now, Darvin.

He did it. The chair-people responded accordingly. The helmsman turned to him and spoke: "Lift achieved."

The ship tore through the roof of Ernest's home. All he could do was fret, cross his arms, and view the screens. One still showed navigation data, but the upper section of the other now offered a head-on view of Earth's looming moon.

"Outer boundary. Point oh-two," the helmsman said.

"OK." Darvin smiled. *Why the hell not? Life is but a dream.* He wondered whether the expired pickles he'd eaten before bed might be to blame.

The ship left the Sol system. Ernest was certain nothing could travel as fast as they appeared to be going, but it made for a spectacular visual. The screen beeped, and a new series of letters scrolled into view.

Issue Communications: Inform P.T.V. Aerie of our arrival time.

He played along with the dream. "Communications, inform the *Aerie* of our arrival time."

Good. Not a defective Darvin. Lilac is pleased.

"My name still isn't Darvin."

He settled back into his chair and watched a speck on the forward screen grow into the smooth, massive form of a ship.

"Sir, *Aerie* signals ready. Advises due haste as pirates have been scanned in the area."

"Uh, right. Helm, take us in. Increase speed as necessary."

"Yes, sir. Point oh-five. Docking preliminaries engaged. ETA: one point four-five minutes."

"*Aerie* reports scan by pirates. Initiating emergency procedures."

Order D.P.V. message transmitted.

"Transmit D.P.V. message. Helm, whenever you're there please."

"Docking, sir."

The private transport vessel *Aerie* quietly swallowed the shuttle whole.

"Dock completed. Shuttle contained. Bay pressurized."

"*Aerie* commander commends you on your speed, sir. Requests your presence topside."

To your right you will find a thin screen. Strap it to your wrist and press the blue light after this message is completed. End of message, Darvin.

He strapped the flexible screen to the underside of his wrist and touched the light. A comforting screen lit with the message: *Report topside. I will guide. Dismiss crew to Rec. It's been a long mission for them.*

Long? *They've only been in existence twenty minutes*, he thought.

Topside, he was welcomed. "Darvin! Welcome aboard." The commander took Darvin's hand in a vice shake. He was a head taller than Ernest, and dark skinned.

A crewmember suddenly went white. "They're coming."

"Damn scientists. Prepare for tach. I want seven," the commander responded.

When defensive shields were activated, Ernest, trying to sound authoritative, said, "That should at least foul up their detection."

"No disrespect, sir, but they're in visual range," sais the crewman. "They don't really need their offensive scanners to blow—"

The commander came to his rescue. "Observation noted. How much time?"

"Eight seconds, on the mark."

"Nav, I want them close and then go!"

"Two secs, on the mark."

The pirates were on them.

"Ride!"

Tachyon drive engaged. The *Aerie* instantly became nothing more than a memory to her pursuers, dwindling out of sensor range.

"Disengage drive. How much did we overshoot?"

"Reading now. Should take us about two weeks to get to Farm Fifteen."

"They can't reprimand us, can they? For being late?" a crewmember spoke up.

"We weren't notified of pirate activity in that system. Farm Fifteen owes us. And where were the Moths? No way they couldn't have received our D.P.A. signal. You did send it, didn't you?"

D.P.A? Ernest was about to say, "The screen told me to send a D.P.V.," when another crewman spoke up, and thus cleared him of any blame.

"Of course. Soon as I got full sensor confirmation."

Another of the technicians began to fret over her console. Ernest noticed red lights dotting her screen, and red seldom meant good. She pushed buttons, finally calling the commander.

"Sir, secondary feed shows signs of malfunction. Minimal containment shield deterioration."

"Rate?" the commander asked.

The technician made calculations, then held up a small pad for perusal. "Very minor at this point. I've detached two roids to handle it."

"Cut feed to a quarter norm. Helm, hold us at a third supraliminal mneme-neuritic velocity until further notice."

Ernest wanted to ask him what several of those words meant and whether they were in any real danger, when his wrist-screen beeped.

Not the time, Darvin, for answers. Retire to Rec Room. I will guide. All questions to be answered at the appropriate time.

He didn't like the notion that the screen knew his thoughts. He thought about saying something to the commander before he left, but saw that the man was engaged with even more technicians. Unnoticed, Ernest made his way off the bridge.

The recreation room was not at all what he expected. Nothing but an oversized honeycomb, twenty or more hexagonal booths mounted a few centimeters above the deck, held in place by spidery prongs that stretched from their tops into the darkness above. Beside each sat a small automated service unit, lit from above by a shaft of light.

Crew signals ready, Darvin.

The whole flickered, and then only three shafts of light, on three units, remained. "What crew?" Ernest asked as he stepped close to the nearest hexagonal booth. The doors on three other booths simultaneously opened and his navigator, helmsman, and communications officer each stepped out. As the doors swung shut again the service unit next to each powered down; the shaft of light above each unit blinked out. The room became shadow, punctuated only by flashes of light from a source that Ernest couldn't see.

Rather than waste time searching for the light (*and after all, if it's a dream I won't find it anyway...*), he nodded to each of the crew.

"Off your high horse, Darvin. No time for it," said the Com officer. She stood about his height and had long, black hair. Ernest couldn't decide whether he liked her or was intimidated.

All three of them wore reflective blue jumpsuits with grey harnesses containing what he assumed might be an assortment of weapons and tools. Not what they'd worn in the shuttle.

"Suit up." An identical suit was tossed to him by the navigator, also female, who could easily have passed as the Com's twin.

Ernest glanced at the helmsman. He wanted to call the man *dangerous*. The man returned Ernest's glance with a curt nod. Ernest stepped into the flimsy suit, and wondered which old television show might have inspired that part of the dream. He took the screen off his wrist until the suit completely sealed itself, sheathing him in the odd material.

"Let's go, Darvin." The navigator led the way into the emptied corridor. They made it to the shuttle bay unseen, which Ernest thought must be unusual aboard a starship. He attributed it to a failure of his sleeping imagination.

Nevertheless, none of the other *Aerie* crew was visible. He queried the wrist-screen about their absence.

Inappropriate.

When he looked up again, the hulking bay doors still weren't open.

"Do it," Com urged, her voice a hiss.

The screen at Ernest's wrist beeped. No one else noticed. *Say following: "This is Darvin ordering command override of topside monitor systems. Identification is Oats and Grain. End, Darvin." Then stand in front of the plate for security screening. Do so now.*

He stepped to the door. It was strange, acknowledging that he was "Darvin," as he said the words. He imagined himself standing upon a mountaintop, fists raised in acknowledgment as he announced to the heavens, "I am Darvin!" And the heavens would simply smile and say, "We know, dear."

A line of light from the security plate traveled over him before a synthetic voice declared, "Screen is affirmative. Darvin override in effect."

The doors opened. His companions rushed in, and sped for the shuttle.

"Move it!"

But they moved too fast for him. The shuttle door opened, and the crew clambered inside, pushing ahead of him. Ernest—Darvin—just managed to leap through as the door closed. Com threw an opaque helmet to him. The navigator and helmsman sealed their helmets to suits, and seated themselves at their consoles. The helmsman stabbed a button. The outer bay doors slid apart, revealing the black essence of deep space.

"How much time?" Helm asked.

"On the one," Com answered. Their voices sounded tinny in Darvin's helmet receiver.

... six... four... two... one.

The small craft shot out of the *Aerie.*

Seconds later, as the shuttle left the ship behind, Darvin turned to admire its massive beauty.

Where are we going? One last glimpse of the P.T.V. *Aerie* filled the screen before the majestic ship exploded in a tight ball of light minus sound. Ragged shards chased the shuttle as it raced ahead of death. The beauty of the sight was overwhelming.

Darvin did what he could: nothing. He caught a whimper in his throat before it could escape.

* * *

"Time to wake up, Darvin." Com's hair tickled his face.

That's right, wake up from this dream. He opened his eyes.

"Here... put your helmet on." She eased it over his head.

"How long?" he asked. He didn't remember going to sleep.

"Out? About an hour. Mira carried you back here."

He tried to put his head together. "Where?"

"We're at the drop off point. Hurry up. Don't know why they let you sleep," she complained.

Helmet sealed, he and Com hunched stern. Darvin used the moments to attempt to piece together what he could. *So the Nav is "Mira."* That was as far as he got.

The navigator and helmsman motioned for them. "Shuttle's on five minute delay, two of which are gone. Get your helmet on," Mira told Com just as her own settled into place. All four of them were suited and sealed.

"Everything set?" Com asked. The helmsman nodded. "Then let's go." She grabbed Darvin's hand and led him to a hatch set in the deck. They climbed through, and into a cramped hold. A pair of smaller dual-sided craft filled the available space. Com opened a hatch on one unit and lay on her stomach in the opened tear-shaped pod; following her lead, he opened the second connected halve's hatch and did the same. Mira and the helmsman frantically climbed into the other two-person pod moments before the hold's bottom slid away. They dropped.

Darvin, on a small screen, could see Com working frantically in her half. She stabbed a button.

"Darvin, what's wrong over there?"

"I... don't know."

"Power up unless you want me to detach. Come on!"

The urgency in her voice made him nervous, but he saw a stud marked *ACTIVATION* below the screen. He hit it.

"Switch command of your pod to me," she ordered.

"I don't know how!"

A look crossed her face. "Below 'activation.' Three switches in a row. Throw them, then the red one beneath."

The helmsman's voice cut in. "What's the delay?"

"Not now." Com cut him off.

Darvin did as he'd been told. Com mumbled to herself. Darvin couldn't decide whether she was more likely speculating on his immediate heritage, or his evolutionary forbears.

The helmsman cut in again. "We're going. No time."

"Go!" Com shouted.

Darvin and Com drifted another moment before their joined pods also shot away from the shuttle. As they departed, it became a smaller version of the *Aerie*, the explosive light mesmerizing with funereal grace.

"Too close," she swore. Darvin imagined the feel of the beads of sweat that dotted her forehead. He remained very still, as if movement might disturb her. The last thing he wanted at that moment was any undue attention.

He wasn't even sure he wanted due attention.

The pods sped along for what seemed years. Darvin became uncomfortable, claustrophobic, flying through space in a souped up tandem coffin, but made use of the time to study the instrumentation. By pressing a small button set into the screen's frame he discovered the ability to change views. One push replaced Com with a star field. Another overlaid a representation of the pod and its course upon the screen. He studied that for a while. The linear trajectory appeared to be carrying them toward a large planet, larger by half than Earth. Another push of the button brought up an informative readout: planetary measurements, atmosphere, dominant environmental system, gravity, average temperature.

He considered having the screen explain the data to him, before deciding that would be a cheat. He wanted to do something, anything, on his own, rather than sacrifice the fleet illusion of control. He clung to that notion, not because it was expected or part of some plan, but because it was what he wished to do.

He got Com's image back. She was beautiful even through the faceplate. Her eyes were closed and he thought she was asleep when, abruptly, they snapped open.

"Stop staring at me."

"I wasn't staring at you. Not for long anyway. How did you know I was looking?"

She changed her screen to course projection.

"It's not as if I was breathing down your neck," he continued, then saw she was ignoring him. He switched his display as well.

He glanced wearily at his wrist. *So much for control.* "OK, screen. Lilac. Whatever you are. Why am I here?"

No response.

After an uncomfortably silent period, Com's voice startled him. "Explain yourself, Darvin."

"You explain."

"You haven't known what you were doing from step one."

"Should have known it was a stupid dream when people started growing out of chairs," he muttered. "I'm ready to wake up now."

Com went on. "I don't care what your excuses or delusions are. You are here to perform, and if this mission is threatened any further Lilac will hold you responsible."

His eyes widened. "You know about Lilac?"

Her expression said that he was a dolt.

"Who is Lilac? I want to see her, want to find out what this is, and I damn well hope this ship's heading for her—"

"I allowed you one threat. A second will not be tolerated."

"And I will not tolerate being used further," he shot back, bolstering his defiance by pressing the stud. The image of Com winked out. Several seconds passed before, on voice only, she informed him that the discussion of his behavior would continue when they landed.

* * *

After the changeover, Darvin started wondering why he still didn't know Com's name. *After all,* he thought, *important characters have names, right?*

They'd been relegated to a smaller shuttle for this leg of the mission, and aside from Com's console, his own screen, the computer tank, and life support, the vessel was bare of instrumentation. It felt stripped clean. Space was utilized to maximum efficiency though, with bundles of equipment secured along the bulkheads. Their tandem pod took up the rest of the room, magnetically locked to the aft deck.

Getting the shuttle had been simple, although he'd become so used to hearing little more than the sound of his own breathing that he had been startled when Com told him to switch his screen to local, a third of the way into the voyage.

In one half of the split screen floated a tiny, bright rectangle. "That's our transfer," said Com. "We dock in five minutes."

As she'd spoken, the section grew to fill the entire screen; the image magnified until Darvin recognized the rectangle as another vessel.

Com explained the procedures: she would perform every necessary task to prep the shuttle; he was to do nothing but wait. *And touch nothing.*

Once berthed and efficiently inventoried, they'd proceeded at maximum drive to Godspeace.

Which they still orbited.

Darvin swiveled his chair to watch Com recheck the gear. Their helmets were off, and her long black hair swung about her shoulders as she moved. Bending over the pods, she pressed three glowing discs on a bulky energy feed unit. The tandem ceased leeching energy from the shuttle's main engines.

She pulled awkwardly at the feed unit, but couldn't get leverage while leaning over a pod. "Darvin, come here." She motioned him to the other side. "Grab that and pull on the count of two."

He took hold. On the count of two they pulled, and the unit rose slowly, until it reached its apex. Darvin held on as it fell backwards against the hinges, trying to slow its descent.

"Let it go, it won't be used again."

The unit crashed to the deck. Extending to ports set flush into the deck were three flexible metallic tubes, each nearly as wide as his neck. He scooted behind the tandem and stepped over the tubes to stand beside her.

"What's your name?"

"Atefeh," she said absently, pronouncing it *Ah-ta-fay*. She crossed back to the bundles of equipment.

"Why do you keep checking those?"

She pointed at a thick ring around the middle of one of the equipment carriage-bags. "Floaters. Without them we might as well never leave the shuttle. When we hit water there'll be no way to haul all this out in time. As is, it should be just enough to get the tandem out. Once we get within three kilos above surface, they'll follow us down. I'll be inside prepping the tandem."

"The floaters will follow the tandem as well?"

"After we've set their follower frequency to match the pod's beacon. This shuttle's going to be moving too fast for us to simply drop from the deck hatch. That would be too risky, even with me as a pilot... and you're pretty worthless, right now."

"Why the need for speed now? I understood when the *Aerie* blew, but we're who-knows-how-far away from there."

"We haven't reached the end yet, Darvin."

"Meaning?"

"That we still have a long way to go, and limited time to do it."

"I'm pretty sure the shuttle can get us wherever you're going quicker than however long it'll take to eject all this and the rest of that," he said.

"This is too big, Darvin."

Arguing made him dizzy, and he silently wished she'd call him something other than "Darvin." The name still felt wrong. He shrugged, then sighed. Atefeh led him back to the control console.

"Strap in. I need you to focus. *This* one is wired as a master bulkhead release; throw it and all those hatches will open so we can eject the bags. Keep your helmet on. Watch this indicator; at three kilometers hit the switch. Shuttle is going on auto, so you don't have to worry about anything else. Course is laid in. We'll impact—pay *attention*, Darvin!—we'll impact in a lake region. As soon as this ship settles throw *that* switch and the one beneath to blow the aft bulkhead. I'll fly the tandem out, and you'll follow me down. The floaters will rest alongside the shuttle, once we splashdown. Stop at each and reset its follower frequency; when you raise the black cover on the top you'll see a keypad. Punch in six-seven-nine-T-E-P-B, and close the cover. Then get in your pod."

"What about the shuttle? We're not going to conceal it or anything?"

"Underwater. And most of it will have been digested by nightfall."

She left him to think about digestion while she worked on the pod. Presently she returned to the console.

"Taking the shuttle in. Five minutes to splashdown. Be quick, Darvin," she advised before locking the course and engaging automatic controls. "Everything's been fed into the computers."

She grabbed her helmet, stepped to the tandem, opened a hatch, and climbed in.

Darvin—not-Darvin?—*honestly-not-sure*-if-not-Darvin sat strapped to his seat while everything happened around him. The craft entered the atmosphere of Godspeace, and he stole fevered glimpses out the forward port in between checking the altitude. He marveled at blue clouds wisped with gold, but then realized it had to be an effect of refracted sunlight.

The three kilometer mark was reached within seconds of breaking atmosphere. He quickly slapped the bulkhead switch, and circular hatches behind each carrier bag blew open. The bags were sucked outward, and from their thick bands short wings of translucent brown extended along a thin metallic framework to provide stability. Each bag dropped, extended, spun and righted itself, then shot after the shuttle in wing-to-wing formation.

He watched the display, wide-eyed.

Five minutes, twenty-three seconds after leaving orbit, as foretold, the shuttle slit the waters of a huge lake. His eyes widened differently, as water gushed through from the blown bulkheads. He struggled against the straps. Something like a drowned gull veered through the water and missed something like a fish outside the forward port. The small craft angle-popped from beneath the water, nearer the shoreline.

The place stank. The smell seeped through the cargo hatches and reeked of primitive influences; it filled his lungs as he leaned over the console and fumbled for the two switches to blow the aft bulkhead. When he'd done so, the polarity locks reversed themselves and the entire aft section fell backwards into the water. *Like the scale of Leviathan*, he thought. The tandem throbbed a second, raised gingerly off the damp surface, and floated end-first out of the opening he'd made for it. Once suspended safely away from the shuttle, it pivoted slowly to the right, and disappeared from view.

Darvin climbed out, sliding a leg into the briny green water, and made quick way to the carrier bags. Their wings had already retracted. As he bobbed in the chest high water, he reset the signal on each, then half swam, half ran around the end of the shuttle. He prayed Atefeh remembered about waiting for him in the tandem.

It was there, but it wasn't alone. He froze; the sudden stop sloshed and splashed water around his arms, and his breath fogged the interior of his faceplate. The tandem was perhaps eight and a half meters away, floating barely a hand's width above the surface. One meter closer to him, a shiny black hump moved through the water, dipped beneath, and reappeared.

He stood terrified, trying to will his body into non-existence. Whatever was making the hump was swimming slowly toward *him*, and he felt as though his chest was either becoming a supernova, or a black hole. Heat radiated and pooled in his fingertips, and he itched.

He brought one arm slowly in front of his helmet so that he could look at the wrist-screen. Something bumped against his thighs. His breath snagged, and he jumped blindly toward the shuttle, doing his best to keep the hump in view.

It slipped beneath the surface, still meters away. A head rose up, directly in front of Darvin's helmet, trailing a mass of unidentifiable vegetation. The eyeless creature opened its mouth, revealing multiple rows of finger-long arrow points, spread across both the upper and lower jaws. Darvin snatched a random object from his suit harness and threw it into the wide maw as he backpedaled. His shoulder hit the side of the shuttle. He swung around, and hauled himself through the aft opening, landing with a splash. Inside the shuttle the water had already reached the depth of his waist. A thick head banged against the opening as it snapped at the air.

He tried to run, lost his footing, wasted no time trying to recover, but kept moving on hands and knees. His shoulder slammed against the edge of the control console.

The creature's head slid underwater. Darvin could feel it bumping along the deck and bulkheads, feeling its way toward him. As he hunkered behind the console, more of the long neck slid in, serpentine. The mottled hide glided easily over the metal.

"Atefeh!"

As the blind creature drew closer to the console he climbed atop the structure. From there he could see that the tandem had also come closer, and that Atefeh had opened a hatch. She fired pellets, and the creature twisted its body in what looked, to Darvin, like agony.

Whatever Atefeh was using looked like a child's plastic drinking straw. Darvin searched his harness for anything similar, and found a promising shape near the small of his back. One wrench tore it from its catch.

He acted as blindly as the monster, aiming the device in as threatening a fashion as he could manage. A stream of marble sized pellets exploded along the side of the oversized mouth. Each impact was accompanied by a wet sizzle and a tendril of smoke.

Suddenly the beast jerked. For a moment Darvin almost thought it seemed as surprised as he was. The long neck thrashed from side to side, churning the water, as more and more of it stretched taut. The head reached the aft hole and its mouth opened, only to clamp down upon the metal edge.

Atefeh shouted at him. "Something's *pulling* it!"

Warily, he walked nearer the massive form. It could have bitten him in half, had it not been too busy to do so.

"Come on!" Atefeh screamed.

Darvin looked at her, stupefied.

"Whatever's pulling that thing is somewhere way out *there*—"

The lake was at least two kilometers wide. Several hundred yards from shore a spot was churning. Darvin looked from the disturbance to the head of the creature as it struggled to hold on.

His amazement was curtailed when the shuttle began to shift and tilt, causing him to slide toward the nonexistent aft bulkhead.

He submerged. He struggled. In his mind he also screamed. His arms and legs flailed in ineffective emulation of the swimming lessons that he—that Ernest—had taken, long ago. As the shuttle tipped again, he broke through the surface. It was easier to stand and walk than to swim in the now shoulder-deep water, so he did.

Atefeh already had his hatch open. He climbed in, buried his head in his arms, and tried to decide whether he was sick enough of the stupid dream to do anything about it.

With the hatch sealed and the pod powered up, Atefeh shot the craft across the water and into a low, rising arc.

Up and away, towards Lilac only knows what, thought whoever the hell he was, at that particular moment.

None of the floaters had been damaged. As soon as their lead signal, still aboard the tandem, moved out, they all silently extended their wings and followed.

* * *

After a while the pattern solidified. He dreamed of returning to something. A return to something he hadn't killed.

They were murderers. On different worlds, large numbers of beings once alive died before Darvin and the woman flew away.

They were locusts. He never understood his supposed position in the organization—Atefeh treated him with contempt often enough—nor its design, if any. There was no sense of a purpose.

Each dazed run left him weaker, drained so that she had only to tug and he would follow, or speak and he would moan.

* * *

On the first world, they simply provided food. It was poisoned.

On the second, they assassinated any on the brink of scientific understanding.

* * *

The third through the fifth became such blurs of guilt and psychological numbness that she nearly yanked his arm out of its socket trying to keep him from opening the airlock.

* * *

On the sixth planet, in its native bifurcate tongue, he finally saw the eyes of one who was about to die in (what was not even) Darvin's name: a frail tri-ped, its chest leg nearly drained of marrow where disease had set in, the surface broken and pustulating.

Darvin had walked into the open space that morning, fully expecting to see several family hutches already feeding at the communal stump. Instead there were bodies.

There were no sounds, no smells, but only the sight of death, and stillness.

The three-legged creatures had no natural enemies, and no predators, so they didn't fear him, or the woman. On the very first day of their visit, the microbes that had ridden his body from star to star began to feast on alien flesh as the creatures rubbed curiously against his unfamiliar form and he palmed, felt, scratched their ruddy silver skin.

They had behaved like cats, with their ears pricked high.

As he walked into the open space that morning, one was still dying, but something within it had not yet died. He almost tripped over it. Even in pain, the creature's eyes remained wide and peaceful; even though the orbs were milky, it saw him and tried some sound. He picked up the small body and, there being nothing else to do, simply stood crying until Atefeh led him away to their latest roundabout transport.

"We are the sleepers, Darvin," she said, "tasked with waking the worlds."

He stared at the serene landscape. "I'm ready to wake up whenever you are."

* * *

Their nineteenth planet was a return to Godspeace.

"I'm pretty tired, Darvin," Atefeh said.

Darvin felt old. Ancient. "Yeah. I've been looking for someplace clear to set down."

She glanced at his face on her screen. Their one constant, between shuttles, had become the weary tandem; he thought of them as coffins for the living.

They flew without the frantic push he'd come to expect, at an altitude five hundred meters over a jagged volcanic region as darkness swathed the surrounding mountains.

"I might've landed in that valley but this area's still active. Very unstable," Atefeh said.

"What's on the other side?"

"A sea. Then from there we get to suitable land. That should be about another ten minutes."

"Why're we here?"

Something large flew through the dim illumination of the tandem lights, ahead of them.

"I'm going to speed up a bit," Atefeh said. "Bring the floaters in tighter." She flipped toggles and pressed buttons. "Back there, that wasn't so good."

"What was it?"

"Don't know. I don't know everything about this planet. Not good though, large flying animals at night. That much I'm pretty sure of."

Inside his helmet, Darvin ran the tip of his tongue around his lips. His eyes went from the screen to the viewport above the nose of his pod. Twice he saw quick, indistinct shapes, flying like darts.

* * *

They survived the landing. They camped on a cliff overlooking the sea.

He looked at the agitated waters. There was no moon around the planet, he knew, but the surface moved in waves. *O' Leviathan, thou art at work, aren't you?*

Atefeh came and stood behind him, near the cliff's edge. She looked at the side of his face, but he ignored her. He'd gotten used to her scrutinizing his features. Her gaze went out to the water, and he thought she might be making an effort to take in what he saw. He doubted she'd see it.

No matter how hard she tried, there never seemed to be beauty for her, nothing to contemplate.

After a bit more silence she said his name. The sound traveled over the cliff and lost itself among the surf.

"A fragile silence. You broke it."

"I wouldn't consider it obscene to be your friend," she said awkwardly.

"I wasn't thinking about friendship," he said.

"After all we've gone through together, we aren't so different, Darvin. My mother used to say—"

"Your mother doesn't exist!" he snapped. "I'm stuck in something that isn't real. Do you understand me? I have no idea who your 'Darvin' is supposed to be, but I'm not him."

She frowned and started to turn away, then paused. "The others will be here soon."

"Who?" He held up his arm and gestured to the wrist-screen. "Lilac?"

She didn't answer. He watched her walk away, and told himself that Lilac must be the most ineffably useless of all MacGuffins; that she (if a she) didn't exist anyway; and that if he ever woke up and got himself stuck in another dream, he hoped he wound up as the bloody Lilac pulling the strings, instead of another Darvin sleepwalking through perpetual, involuntary slaughter.

He looked back down at the wrist-screen. *If not Lilac, then who?*

Then he knew: the old navigator, Mira, and her dangerous helmsman. Forgotten characters introduced part of the way through his story. Something about guns and mantelpieces skipped through his thoughts before rage at this infernal game in which he was caught, this macabre reunion of life and death, chased it from his mind.

How was it that he still knew he was someone else? After changes upon changes, he was more or less the same.

He snapped at her again. "You don't exist!"

"What are you trying to do, Darvin?"

"I am *not* Darvin. This is not my life!"

Then she blinked. Or perhaps he blinked, and she momentarily got stuck in the not-seen. Either way, it lasted barely a second... then she was back, eyes as wide as the tri-ped's had been, but full of fear. They were locked on Darvin.

Atefeh sat very still, as if afraid to move. Every aspect of her was a request for help, for someone to rescue her from the dangerous madman who would destroy worlds by blinking or waking up. But hadn't she also told him they were sleepers, tasked with waking worlds?

Help. It was as if that one word became her single point of existence.

His ears rang. He focused, trying to hear what, if anything, she might say next, but the only audible sound that broke through his concentration was an insistent beeping from the wrist-screen. He looked at it.

Lilac has instructed me as to your situation. Is this real to you?

"Oh, bloody hell. I was sitting at my computer, for God's sake! Fully conscious, *aware* of the passage of moment to moment, and in one of those moments I noticed my machine. When that moment became the next, a frigging spaceship equipped with a crew of three, and a fully operational universe—which I evidently missed the first fifteen minutes of—was growing out of my computer. Completely normal for all of them, but me, me, I've not seen anything real since I got here! What in hell's a *Darvin*? Atefeh doesn't know that she has no past. She was bloody well going to tell me about her mother."

She is highly disturbed by your tirade.

"I'm highly disturbed by a bucket-load of this place. She was gone for a second. What—"

We will never be said to not try new things. This one was stable beyond question. You forced doubt upon her and destabilized her scenario.

"*What* was stable?"

The dream. You are expected to know how to behave in your own dreams, Darvin.

"So I'm really dreaming?" Tears pooled in his eyes.

A pocketful of universes, Darvin. Some of them are always a dream.

He felt a jolt of fear as Atefeh flickered again.

"No! Leave her. Just leave her alone." She was trembling violently.

"*Darvin?*" Her voice was barely able to remain afloat long enough to be heard.

Part of him wanted to go to her, to hold her because he was human, even if he wasn't sure what she was. He didn't move. "I can't, I'm sorry... I won't stay here. Believe me, if there was any other way—"

"Darvin?"

"No. I can't keep doing this." He desperately wanted her not to blame him, not because he liked her, and not because she was a woman, but because she believed her universe was real, and he was about to rip that away.

The last of anything he saw before she was sucked/ripped/coruscated away was that the word for her had changed. *Help* had been uncomfortable yet oddly reassuring; it made him feel he wasn't quite so alone. She became another word before she, then the entire universe, washed away. The word was *Pain*, and the promise and warning in it weren't directed at him particularly. What she'd become told him there was no such thing as rest. The universe did not rest. The universe was a shark, always swimming so that it didn't suffocate.

Life without ceasing, and worlds without end—even at the end.

* * *

Niimu was ready for him.

"Are you now or have you ever been a life form?" The checkmaker regarded the he-soul as on countless times before, and during, and present. The accumulation of life after life deposited itself in the universal *I-have-been-here-before*. All the souls in line ahead and behind had been him, and he them, *ad infinitum.* Eventually the soul would be everything that consciousness might possibly present, he-soul and she-soul and *other-for-which-a-pronoun-is-insufficient*-soul... but for now, he was holding up the line.

Niimu did something that wasn't exactly clearing one of its throats, and asked again, "Are you now or have you ever been a life form?"

Darvin was gone. Ernest was absent. The dream, at last, was over, and it felt pretty good to wait a bit before another leg of sleep.

The he-soul voiced no words. It glowed a bit. It closed its eyes.

Eternity could not be delayed forever, but as long as it stood here there would be neither angels to worry about nor demons to avoid. Only Niimu, who was fixed.

How sad. Fixed

No matter what, no matter what, there will always be another go around.

The A Team

Jesus made the best chocolate chip cookies. Vishnu made the bread. Buddha handled the punch, and of Shiva, 'tis better the less is said. The Great Spirit sat at the head of the table. Mohammed prepared everyone spiced tea. Moses kept bringing word of the world below; finally, everyone bowed their heads. Didn't pray for lasting peace, didn't demand pious dread. This grand celestial gathering sent thoughts of fasting instead. No gorging on indolence and foolishness, no dripping red helpings of greed. Quite full off fear and avarice (and deception is why most wound up dead). Supping on evil causes conniption fits guaranteed to shred a peaceful bed. And the dreams of these humans, Moses reported, the dreams, he perplexedly said...

...of those sad mistreated things, 'tis better the less is said.

"There's always more," their dreams scream and scream. "Control, consume and confound!" A steady supply of money is preferable to hallowed ground. "Drink and eat and never need, but always want instead." Have unwise sex, and seek chemical twists, to balm the wounds by which you're led.

The celestials fell silent. Jesus stood, decision made. Buddha joined him too. Botha Dish of the African plains completed the trio three. What good's a party in the celestial rounds with noisy neighbors below? They rappelled to earth, clad all in black and packs, the mission abundantly clear: spread less fear not more cheer, and get back to the work of the day. Their descent was watched from above till the clouds swallowed them up and The All sat back to lament. Another thousand years, as it gazed at the pile of warm cookies, before any returned to fill up that plate, but

this is the role great spirits play, and of that what more
is there to say?

Mini Me's:

So a Congressman walks into a bar with his penis hanging out. There's no joke.

Wanda laughed often at Fred, but in reality she was Masengill, warrior priestess and tax preparer, battling Thoom and Vichyswah on faraway lands. She had no time for little men and their discussions of the day-y...hey, wait now, dessert menu. OK.

"You little punks think it's OK to tease an old man, do you?!" said Renfield. "That's OK, I've got a much older man to deal with you," he shouted, unlocking the lid on Vlad's casket once more.

More and more piled on her until the red sky was barely visible and her arm barely touched the air. Their bodies smelled and clogged her senses with heat. The image of Justine flashed through her mind. She fought like a maniac, her entire body a spiked club. "None may touch Susie Saindon!" she bellowed, smashing free and standing ready among mangled bodies, her chest heaving, her eyes feral, teeth bared. She would never leave Justine. Never.

"Peter?"
"We've never left, Wendy."
"Where have you been?"
Pan smiled.
"You naughty boy! You've been living in my knickers all this time," Wendy realized, aware for the first time where her insatiable sensuality came from.

From outer space it came, but it was just looking for directions. Thirty-foot tall asexual quadripeds make the army nervous. Because I was riding shotgun in its ship, I'm stranded here now. I'm about 2 micons tall, so don't look for me. That feeling when you're at work and you want to get the hell out of there? That's me. Two reasons: I've gotta do something to keep from getting bored, and it's hard as hell to get your attention. Blogtharagnatius should regenerate in about another sixty years. Till then, don't you have another meeting to go to, hmm?

"The only evidence I need of Intelligent Design," said Senator Bloodaxe, unsheathing his crusted blade and laying it before the security dogs for evidence of illegal killing, "is what I have seen with my own eyes."

"But, Senator," someone said from the throng of pelt-clad reporters, "isn't it true you were once a staunch supporter of the scientific prin—"

"Who said that!" Bloodaxe raged, grabbing up the sword that had sent scores of unbelievers to undeserved glory and swinging it round.

The news crews were used to his rages and smoothly raised shields. The senator calmed.

"Senator, it's been rumored," came a crisp, female voice from beneath the turtle's back of shields, "that you yourself have killed angels and that this conversion is purely political."

Bloodaxe grinned at their fear. "Face Bloodaxe, wench," he said, eyes scanning. "Taste congressional steel."

Movement issued from the rear. Reporters parted until she stood before Bloodaxe (R) from Indiana. The huge man's eyes narrowed.

"I am Kurok, daughter's daughter of Couric," which sucked balls because politicians hated a reporter with something to prove.

"Bring it, wench."

Kurok approached. "Today is a good day to cry..."

Only in an alternate reality would I make you cry. Only among a billion other multiverses will you find me away from your side. But *here*, I am yours. Believe.

"Leave, Joe, just get the hell away! I don't need you, I don't need your lies, I don't need your ignorant ways! Get out!!!"

He took a step toward her. "Don't think you ain't gon' miss me."

"Joe, you know that old joke about with every shot I take? Prick, I've been taking lessons." She didn't pull the gun to let him know life suddenly wasn't a game. He weighed it in his eyes. He charged. She pulled the trigger. Twelve years decisively came to an end.

Sometimes decisions aren't made, they're caught up to.

The tower's stairwells were usually deserted. Every once in a while the old building's huge roaches wound up dead in the crook of a step. Rounding the 9th floor landing, Dilby the Tracker spotted one. A little spear stuck out of its side...

Rounding the 9th floor landing, Dilby spotted one: another cockroach with a tiny spear sticking out of its side. The wee men were getting sloppy. He bagged it and thought he caught a quick sight of blue. He whirled. A small blue body lunged from the upper landing, a broad knife between its teeth...

A small blue body lunged from the upper landing, a broad knife between its teeth. It wore the red hat and breeches of an elder warrior, with flowing and matted white beard. Dilby swatted it away in time, but there was no swatting the mass of blue bodies that suddenly appeared behind it. The elder pinged off the wall and stood shakily, wiping blood from its mouth as the surge waited. It looked Dilby in the eye. "Live Smurf or die!" it shouted. Blue bodies thundered past its raised fist.

Dead Smurfs. Everywhere. The stench of it...the officer in charge had been on the force nineteen years and had never once mourned as he did now. The tracker, Dilby, had survived, but kept mumbling over and over, "They came by the hundreds...stomped and crushed, they kept coming." White warrior hats lay like haiku petals...until the officer, Able Murtaugh, came to one slightly different. Blood had dried a lock of blond hair to it. Murtaugh dropped to his knees...

Murtaugh dropped to his knees, squishing a few half dead Smurfs but it didn't matter. He pinched up the white hat with the blood around the rim. Their queen. They were nothing without their queen. And he was nothing without her. Forbidden love was a meaningless secret now and his life was over. He rounded on the tracker and drew his weapon...

He rounded on the tracker and drew his weapon. "Rogue!" shouted another officer, drawing his own weapon. Guns pointed at Murtaugh. One gun pointed at Dilby.

Dilby regarded Murtaugh with sudden clarity. "You loved her," he said, "her?" Dilby stood. "She was death itself, breeding with every one of these—" he kicked a pile of Smurfs toward Murtaugh. A few bounced down the stairs. "They're everywhere now! We are the dominant species, we!" said Dilby, pounding his heart.

Murtaugh's finger hadn't left the trigger. "Stand down," a junior officer warned from the landing above. The cramped stairwell guaranteed a ricochet bloodbath.

"Smurfs are a disease!" shouted Dilby. "Humanity is the cure! We will cleanse this world—"

"Live Smurf or die!" screamed officer Able Murtaugh and whipped the gun to his own temple. The shot pierced the wall. The moment before he fired and fell he thought he saw a foot twitch, a small white shoe with heels, and he realized that his dead body would squish her. The final thought of officer Able Murtaugh, decorated officer of the Civil Police Force, and never to be known by any, not even himself, was 'Damn.'

Murtaugh's clothing was sticky with crushed Smurf jelly. A young M.E. made the joke about slapping peanut butter on him. They wheeled Murtaugh's body outside. The medical examiner's assistant was pretty. If he was lucky he'd be able to skim some of this aphrodisiacal jelly off and maybe get it refined by the Chico Brothers, who didn't exist but who made the finest highly illegal Smurf-caine available. Dead Smurfs got geeks laid. "This was terrible," he said to his assistant. She looked somber. "Yes," she said. He handed her a shovel to scoop up the beginning of what he hoped would be a Smurftastic night.

He would hate himself in the morning.

Spiderweb Tea

A few feet from the Cajun Queen's trailer Tim hesitated and looked at the ground for pebbles to grind into the dirt. Beneath the high moon he slipped himself an unlit cigarette. Every fourteen year old and-up this side of Liberty Mill had claimed to have stood this spot. The pool hall men got their kicks calling her "Slow Burn," but who cared what they said? She was the most perfect thing in Mississippi, in town one summer week with the traveling carnival.

One of the retarded kids had tried to say she'd let him see her naked last year. Before he got out "Swear to God!" he was laughed away from the circle. Tiny Dempsey, whose church mama never let him anywhere near anything fun, swore the same till he was blaspheming and red-faced.

Most believed chances improved if you pretended to know poetry.

The boy silently recited the only poem he admitted he liked, even though it had weird names. He'd found it in the library thinking limericks meant dirty jokes.

So I and my love Liadan
Should sleep together without sin
While any layman on the earth
Would boast of what that chance was worth;
Though I and my love Cuirithir
Had practiced virtue for a year
Left together for one night
Our thoughts would stray before daylight.

Title was "Ordeal by Cohabitation." An English teacher's way of saying something dirty. His English teacher was pretty, so this poem stayed in his mind.

A lamp glowed through folded sheet drapes. He glanced toward the carny. The amusement rides sat dark. They looked mean. Every now and again he imagined hearing voices.

Then he felt foolish.

"Tim." Talking around his cigarette like that he felt like J. Dean; he stood a touch straighter. The silky red scarf she'd given him earlier that day after the Amazing Grande had called for a volunteer from the crowd bulged his pocket. He'd made certain to be at the front and hopped up there before Grande had finished saying, "And now, if I may, a vol—"

Then Tim Burrow stood there right next to the Cajun Queen.

Amazing Grande's lovely assistant.

Karen.

Timothy Burrow gazed over the gathered men and women, over the agitated sea of young boys, heart frying as the Queen led him to the magician. She touched Timothy at his wrist with the tips of her fingers. And never left his side. If he had died without saying his morning prayers it would have been all right because as long as you die with a smile Heaven takes you, and if he fell unconscious she would have to mouth to mouth him—

"You all right, boy?"

"Yessir."

"What's your name then?"

"Timothy," he said.

"Little Tim, do you believe in the power of transmogrification?"

She wore a sparkly bathing suit; her legs stuck all the way out. "I'm not sure."

"Then let's make believers out of everybody here." An oversized black cloth draped a small table. "Over there you see an empty, opened box." The magician held to the front of the stage while the Cajun Queen led Tim to the box. "Check it, boy, and assure these discriminating folks of no false bottoms, no mirrors, hit on it if you got to, no tricks at all, just a plain and simple box."

She handed it to Timothy. Of course he didn't say anything about the mirrored false bottom. He made a show of looking inside and shaking it, then looked directly into her eyes, knowing he had to be attractive by now—hell, he was wearing cologne and his best shirt—and he husked the words, "Just a box, ma'am." She did a little flip of her hand over the box and swung her arm out as though dropping seed. The audience clapped.

Amazing Grande picked up a matching box, twirled it, and held it out. "Two empty boxes, solid wood."

He caught the rubber chicken the Queen tossed to him.

"And here we have tonight's dinner—"

From the crowd: "She cook it I'll eat it!"

Amazing Grande ignored this, saying to Timothy, "Give me something you can part with, something personal." Of course it would be a key. Folks who attended magic shows always brought keys just in case.

"I got this key," Burrow said, digging in his pocket.

The silky red scarf entered like a sign. It hung loosely around her forearm. One wavy tug and she held it free and clear, took it delicately at the corners, flipped it back to front, then held her hand out for his key. She had to smile for the act, but it was no accident the perfume from her skin was on that scarf.

She rolled the key into delicate folds before tying the scarf at both ends. The Amazing Grande tied this to the rubber chicken, which was quickly transmogrified by placing it in his box, locking the lid, making intense hand gestures and, *Hupspa!*—that was his word—throwing open the inspected box that had been repositioned atop the table. A live chicken was inside. It wore a red scarf around its neck. In Grande's box: nothing. And inside the scarf--

"Ta-daaa!" trilled the Cajun Queen. Even though her hand was up and a hip out, her eyes weren't on anything.

--inside was a key.

Under the noise of applause she whispered without moving her lips for the boy to stay after the show because it wasn't his key. They let him keep the scarf. It wasn't the same one. It smelled like a chicken.

He left the stage with a huge grin, without a glance toward his cheering friend.

Here in the moonlight Burrow wondered if he was out of his mind. Ten steps. Her trailer was right there.

So he moved, eyes straight on her door, a straight line, brain locked so tight as the raggedy door moved closer he completely forgot why he was there. He took the cracked steps of that trailer and only then realized how big it was. It was a church. He knocked, and glanced left and right before knocking again. He glanced backwards. Then felt vibrations. The Cajun Queen walked buck naked toward the door for Timothy Burrow with smeared lipstick from where she'd been washing for bed and she was going to look down and see...

...a lump in his pants.

He whipped the scarf out and stood tall.

"What is it?" she called.

"I," he said to the peeling wood. "I'm not sure you remember me." He wore the same shirt as earlier. He'd bathed.

"Wrong thing to say to a lady's door at night."

A honeysuckle voice, a magnolia, a plate of grits and cheese—

The door opened. She wasn't naked but she shivered his soul like dry ice. She was beautiful. She wore loose satin with lace in nice places, redder than the scarf.

"You smoke them things?" She wrinkled her nose.

He'd forgotten the cigarette hanging from the corner of his mouth. Reminded, he called forth James Dean. "Oh, naw." He flicked it off to the side. "I come to give you back your scarf," he said and thrust it forward.

"Shouldn't you be home? Yeah, I remember you. Nearly broke your neck jumping on the stage."

He remembered it as athletic. "Figured you might want this back since the material's fine."

"Wouldn't imagine handsome boys have much use for silk scarves." She moved a half step back.

The next morning, when he told his best friend about it, the response, "She really said that?" made the world a little clearer.

Timothy nodded. His friend's father worked a small apple orchard. They sat high in a good climbing tree.

"Then she said thank you, good night, and closed the door. Smiled at me a little," said Timothy.

"I think you might be the one this year."

Timothy shook his head. "Ain't that easy. Cajun Queen could have anybody. I gotta make her see why it should be me."

"You got a plan?"

"Like maybe she could be walkin' the creek and fall in and panic after she sees a cotton-mouth. I jump in and have her out."

"What if she can swim?" Luther asked, reaching for a pale red apple.

"You ever seen her swim? No."

"You could tell her you want to take her for a cola."

"I'd have to go out to do that," huffed the boy. "I'm to walk up to her, she'll say yes? I need to figure a way she'll know I'm sincere."

"Betcha Joe's thinking the same thing."

"Joe? She ain't desperate and he ain't even fourteen yet, he's just tall."

"He was talkin' how he'da beat you to the stage if his sister hadn't been next to him."

Joe's sister, Merle, was always on the lookout for Tim. "Joe's no problem."

But that afternoon Joe beat him to the stage, not knowing Timothy hadn't intended to try. It was too soon. Instead what Tim did was spot the crowd for real competition, figuring he knew the Queen's tastes enough to say no to the quiet geeky kids, the straight laced ones, the silly ones whose eyes bugged like fish every time she bent, the coloreds and the flat out ugly ones. Didn't leave too many, and of those a good portion wouldn't have the nerve to approach her and a better portion would simply lie and say so. None of them had counted the days to the carny's arrival or personally ironed all their shirts, as well as practiced their enunciation so as not to appear hicks. He'd fallen instantly in love with the Cajun Queen two years ago, when he spotted her siren eyes crying behind one of the colorful tents. She never looked up to see him. At twelve years old, his only instinct was to leave her be.

Couldn't help but fall in love. But the Cajun Queen, while wearing shiny red lacy stuff, had told him he nearly broke his neck trying to get onstage. If that was how she saw him then he was just a boy.

Timothy found a spot where the crowd thinned enough for him to think. Being in a daze was too deep in thought for his liking. He found a bench. A mother sat on the other end, smoking a nub of cigarette. She anxiously dabbed the hollow of her neck with a thick wad of napkins. He imagined her plowing through the crowd and firing off a shot that might hit Joe just before Tim tackled her a few feet from the Cajun Queen.

He watched the woman. She finally crushed the nub beneath a purple sandal. Never made a move to reach down her blouse and pull out a gun, though she did stuff her napkins in there. He'd seen his own mother fish two fingers in hers once and whip out money and a grocery pad.

"Something wrong there, boy?"

"No, ma'am."

"OK then."

Loud applause meant the Amazing Grande had completed another act of transmogrification. Next performance wouldn't be for another half hour. Timothy considered a meandering stroll to the trailers where he might accidentally cross her slow, sultry path.

He veered instead to the Ferris wheel, having glimpsed Merle. Merle was usually all right except when she insisted on talking about their life together.

She saw him and waved him on. "You didn't have to run all the way over here. Where you been? I saw you yesterday. Called after you but you were walking around all hypnotized." The kids got in line for the wheel. "You got up on stage like a big shot." She smiled. "Thought you might break your neck."

He shrugged. "I think I wanna say," said the boy, "I made the trick for him. You see how expert I was?"

"Joe went up there a little while ago," she said with obvious scorn.

"Where you wanna go when we get off this?" he asked, struck by the impulse to spend the afternoon with her. It would take his mind off the Queen.

He snuck out that night without the cigarettes and biked to the park. No guards or dogs. He quietly climbed the high wire fence and quietly dropped down. Late night air jazzed him. That was definitely a signal she'd given him last night. No other way to see it. He went directly to her door this time, or as directly as the most shadowed route took him. Her lamp was on. He took a deep breath, took a swallow, and knocked. He immediately studied his feet.

Why's her light always on so late?

The door opened and she didn't even ask who it was. "You out again?" She had an untied robe over the red thing. She stood there looking down at him, her long brown hair unkempt, no makeup on her face. "You didn't jump up there today, so you must not have anything for me."

He had plotted a variety of ways where saying this meant she'd have to say that. He even wore a tie.

She smiled at him. It helped with breathing but he still couldn't find any of his memorized words.

"What's your name again?" she asked. The Cajun Queen was eighteen. His eyes followed her left leg to see if it would back up again.

"Timo—" He coughed into his hand. "Tim Burrow."

"That's what smoking cigarettes'll do to you. Here, come on in, I'm getting a chill, 'fore someone sees you."

"I don't want to intrude."

She put hands on satin hips. "That's likely the stupidest thing I ever heard at night." She moved to one side and presented the path to glory. He entered, good space between them else he'd have brushed against her, and took in the simplicity. There was a small bureau for her makeup where the lamp sat, thin brown curtains over the two windows, floral rug beside the bed, a stack of thin books on a nightstand, small refrigerator, and a bed that barely looked big enough for one to stretch. Every story he'd heard about incense and red scarves, oils, beads, mirrors and the size of the bed burned away on the spot. She closed and locked the door.

"Have a seat." The only chair was the one at the dressing table. He sat there with his reflection in a small mirror, feeling like *it* was looking at *him*. Then she walked by and sat on the edge of the bed. "What brings you out here, Tim?"

"I dunno." He tried very earnestly not to look directly at her. She sat like a tomboy. She leaned forward, resting her elbows on her knees and her chin in her hands.

"You ever been in a woman's room this late?"

He shrugged and caught himself about to mumble, "My mama's," but stopped.

"You got to ease up. I'm not a spider and you're not a fly." He pulled his eyes from the floor. She was grinning at him.

"Ok," he said.

"First off, my name is Karen and that's all you ever call me."

"I know. Karen. I think it's a pretty name."

"Thank you. How old are you? When's your birthday?" she asked quickly.

"January seventeenth, nineteen fifty-five. Fourteen."

"Good." She patted the bed for him to cross. "I know boys talk and I know what you come here expecting. Don't think about looking hurt or innocent. I'm the Cajun Queen, and most you probably heard is lies, which you'll be mouthing yourself when we head back to Orleans."

"I wouldn't do that," he said.

"You're going to remember me for the rest of your life, but come next year don't look for me 'cause I'll look right through you. Tonight you're going to talk to me. 'What, just talk!?'—and I'm going to give you a kiss. I think I might like kissing you. You got girlish lips. And you blush easy! I knew I'd like you."

Something, though, made him frown. It was almost like she didn't love him.

"What's wrong?"

He didn't know what possessed him. "This ain't right." He expected he might as well head for the door.

She shoved him backwards. Almost as soon as he hit the bed her hair framed his face. He gazed up that stream of fine, soft straw into her smiling face and thought for a moment he was going insane: the face was getting bigger and bigger. He didn't blink until the hair brushed his temples and he realized she was lowering her lips.

"Uh-uh, don't open your mouth, dear," he heard.

And she kissed him. A peck. The veil of hair lifted. She was about to speak. He was transfixed on her lips.

"Darlin' Tim, this ain't even legal."

He hadn't considered the law. "They can arrest me for feeling like this?" he said, his words remote and fluffy.

"No, honey. When they get you for feeling good that's when it's time to let go."

He murmured something unintelligible. *So this is what it was like to feel Christ's love.* Lazily he said, "Karen..."

She dropped beside him. "Hmm?"

"Nothin'. I just wanted to say your name. You got a middle name?"

"Yes."

"You gonna tell what it is?"

"No."

"Why?"

"Because you'll ask what my last name is. Sit up, I want to show you something." She picked up a stack of books. "These are my secrets."

"Yeah, but everybody's seen them."

"Not hardly." She spread them out so he could read the individual titles.

"They're poetry," he said.

"You always say the most obvious things. We're sitting here looking at them, of course it's poetry. Pick one."

"Why?"

"I need to see how alike we are."

This was a test where they watch you like a hawk without telling you what you're supposed to do.

It seemed simplicity was the key, so without too much hesitation he picked the book with the least decorative cover, which was also the thickest book. He flipped it to read the back jacket.

"Up and coming poet...*Spiderweb Tea*, her latest astonishing collection..."

"I got that a couple years ago," she said.

He thought he should hand it to her and await judgment but she ignored him to stack the other books away. "Take it home. Just make sure you bring it back."

"How alike are we then?"

The suspense was fierce but she smiled happily, and suddenly the weight left and he felt fireworks in his head and stomach. He clenched his jaw to keep from looking silly but the smile broke through anyway, which made her laugh.

"You ever read poetry?"

He answered truthfully.

"This won't change anything for you then. Things don't change much usually."

"But boys grow to be men, don't they?" He didn't want to be a pool hall man.

"Mostly." The next hour they exchanged questions, with him finally giving free answers without having to weigh, feint or counter. She'd even turned off the lamp at one point so that they were whispering in the pale moonlight filtering through her parted curtains. She would rub his hair or rest her hand atop his shirt buttons, and kissed him twice more, the last kiss so soft and full he wasn't ashamed in the least about his pants. Later, but not by much, he carefully climbed into his bedroom window. The rush of excitement was still on him and he had to read.

He got in bed, got out his flashlight, and turned to the first page.

T-Rex's arms being so close to its body made it perfectly suited for texting, but after billions of years of dinosaur inhabitation there are no traces of dinosaur technology simply because the dinosaurs were smart enough to use biodegradable tech.

The Aliens Cloned Trent Darcell

Here's the thing: don't jump out an airplane without first making sure there's no UFO under you, 'cause those suckers will swoop on you in a heartbeat, and then there's the butt probes, the nut 'trodes, the nasal lubes, the ear drum licklers, the blind taste tests and the nipple surprise.

I know this because I'm watching one insert things into me right now. Actually, not so much me. I'm the clone.

Here's what I see: in a bar fight, aliens would get their asses handed to them. Poor little grey Poindexters couldn't beat a girl off a boy band, and I know boy bands 'cause I used to be in one.

I'm Trent Darcell.

Any psychics picking this up will need to call the Enquirer on my behalf. Trent Darcell is not at an undisclosed location in Australia, no matter how they like to make jokes about 'Outback Mountain.' Stupid gay cowboy movie. Right now just about every orifice I have has something blinking sticking out of it, and I do not enjoy it in the least, so, no, Trent Darcell is not gay.

Not that there's anything wrong with that.

OK, so Seinfeld did that, but I make it fresh again.

They look exactly like what everybody thinks, because that's who's been coming here the past umpteen years. They've got pictures lining the walls: Telly Savalas, '78; Hugh Hefner, '94; both Bushes George, '98 and 2008 respectively; David Bowie, '71, '77, '80, '84; Monroe, '58.

Of course, a group photo with the King, '92.

Deal with it.

They got people in pictures in French costumes, but those are probably people from the Revolution. Trent Darcell failed history. Marie Antoinette, Marie

Osmond, what's the difference? There's some black dudes, there's some Jap dudes, this scientist I swear I've seen before 'cause he's got this cool wheelchair and robot voice, like 'I am Locutus of Borg,' but more mechanical, and some old-school politicians. Like Nixon. I recognize him. These little grey fucks've been zipping earth forever, man, like they ain't got shit else to do. Trent Darcell is supposed to be skydiving! Not watching Trent Darcell get anal probed ten times better than that faggot Diamond Lane. Little London prick says boy bands are dead; says Lip Patrol is a bunch of 40-somethings trying to project teenage anguish. Teenage anguish drives, man. Drives everything. Even little grey alien fucks have teenage anguish. Trent Darcell has a private air fleet. Little West End twit can't say the same.

I'm supposed to learn from watching Trent Darcell. From what I understand, clones are given this genetic blip so they can broadcast to each other sometimes, which is cool 'cause I get to have sex with starlets and back-up dancers. Back-up dancers put out poon for the ages. There's this one named Kimmie gave me head *while* I was burying the bone—tell me how that's possible!

He's a lucky bastard.

When they get tired probing for the day we're popped in the same cell but separated by a clear half-wall it'd be too much trouble climbing over. Trent usually doesn't feel like climbing anyway.

"Rougher than usual today, man?"

"Shut the fuck up."

Dumb ass called me Thing One when they dropped me out the vat and introduced me to him, so I call him Thing Two. How I came from somebody so stupid I'll never know.

"You cried today, man. You do every day but today was epic." I waited. He didn't respond. "You cried like a leedle—"

"Shut up!" he spat. Literally. Our chronic shame was Trent Darcell was a wet mouth. Couldn't give an interview without sharing saliva, so he licked his lips all the time because some of the black dudes did it and looked cool.

"Listen, man, Spock (is that cool or what?) told me I'd be out of here soon, so maybe you wanna act like we're fam and I pass along any messages, y'know?"

"You're a copy."

"You ain't?"

"Trent Darcell—"

"Has never composed a melody, has never written, never read, can't truly sing and certainly never thought in ways that are unique and amazing. Dude, my new brain is the shit. Check this out—" And I hit him with my latest song. I've got three albums ready to drop, in my mind. To do justice to them, though, I'll have to go solo.

So his mouth is hanging when I finish the a capella and do a sweet beat box fadeout on my chest.

"Came up with that last night when you wouldn't talk to me. Hey, didn't mean to make you cry. That's a beautiful song, ain't it? You'd never have done that." Spock just happened to be walking by. He gave me the thumbs up. My head bobbed with the appreciative nod. "All right. Look, man, it's cool. I'm you, right, so it ain't like you'll be missing out. It's a two point-oh world, man. I pod, I phone, I am. Hell, they might have some three-tittied Kirk chick out in space for you. I'm probably the one getting the short end. Earth, man." I shrugged. "That's like going down on somebody when their hotter sister coulda gone down on you."

He grabbed hold of a knob grafted to his chest. I saw the look in his eye.

"Aw, man, don't try that again. Spock? Spock!"

He came padding back in that soft sissy-run aliens have. Spoke perfect English.

"What?" he said.

Like they're not supposed to know English? Even Trent Darcell knows enough Spanish to order beer and get laid.

I pointed.

"Dammit, Trent, leave that alone!" Spock said. Spock looked at me. "He knows all that does is hurt him, right? You know all that does is hurt you, right? It's not like that's a mind control thing. It's a shunt. OK? Leave it alone. We'll need that tomorrow."

"Three-tittied women, Trent."

"Where?" said Spock, the little gill flaps under his chin puffing with excitement. Universal love, man. Little dude thought I might have found something in the library he hadn't looked up yet. We were cool and all but I didn't have time to humor him. Trent was about to do it. He yanked that port, screamed, feinted, sprayed blood on the way down, and didn't wake up in time to see me off.

First place I hit was Sydney 'cause, hell, they were going to print it anyway. Appeared in a club at the downcrest of pumping and didn't get recognized till I told these two ladies to get on stage with me and try to keep up. We did a half hour set straight out of Lip Patrol's videos and the ladies stayed so synched with me people swore later the whole thing'd been choreographed. Trent Darcell doesn't play instruments but I told somebody I needed a guitar, and wherever they found one at three in the morning I don't know, but it was red, slick, and came with a fast-moving roadie who hooked me up and leveled me out so tight I hired him on the spot.

I played clunky at first and hammed it up till I learned the sounds, then I played till 4 a.m., giving these lucky bastards half the glorious album I planned to drop next week. My dancers just stared slack-jawed at me. I think I had my picture taken more that night than my entire career. Camera phones stuck out like lighters to capture the ephemeral essential, which on the spot became the title of the album.

The morning news said it all: Who IS Trent Darcell? When I left that club I got on a plane, got home to L.A., phoned my sky diving pilot who hadn't wanted to be implicated in Trent Darcell's likely death to let him know everything was cool. He was unemployed but everything was cool. I didn't give a single interview, which drove them crazy. I pushed porn off the internet for almost an hour. Blogs, news, posts, searches. Who the hell was Trent Darcell, 'cause no way was he the man from Lip Patrol.

"Trent, you wanna take this call?" My roadie-manager-main man kept my guitar clean and my calls blocked. This one was on the private band line. Rang with our breakout song's ringtone. "Girrrlllll," boom boom boom boom, "slap my beats—"

"With yo teats," I adlibbed. "Put it through."

"Trent, what the fuck, man?" said Taylor. "Hell's all this?"

"What?"

"Talent, motherfucker! What the fuck, you tryin' to leave the band? Make us look bad?" He sounded like he was in tears. "We coulda made that album, man! I can't even get on Leno now, man. I fucked Hilton last night and I can't even get on Leno! Leno, you pasty bastard! Everybody wants to know how the hell Trent is suddenly popping off like a rabbit on Vialis! You're the number three man, man, you're the safe one! I'm the brooder, Tawan's the black dude, Tommie's the bad boy, you're Trent: you know the steps and get the milfs. You're the milf-man!"

"Step into the light, brother," is all there is to say. Band's over. Mothers I'd like to fuck, huh? As of now, mothers and daughters better work tandem.

"You can't break up the band! Three's don't break up the band!"

Ain't nothing worse than a whining lead singer.

"Taylor—" Wait. I'm picking up images, my hand gropes the air for comprehension, I'm frowning— "Gotta let you go," and when I disconnect I drop the phone in the koi pond and sit to collect myself a minute. Canoli the Roadie of Doom waits ready to fiddle and adjust me as necessary. I nod him off. "I'm good, man. It's a sunny day. Ogle groupies." Canoli's handsome enough to get laid on his own, but fly fishing within my sphere, hey, teach a man to fish and he'll eat for life. The two ladies lounging around my reflecting pool were pure Marlin, man. Too beautiful for relations without sprinklings of Darcell's pixie dust. Tranced so deep now everyday was Never Never Land and Sydney, Australia was just a dream.

I'm not sure what I saw but it felt like a man asking another man for sex with the kind of anticipation a kid saves for the end of a rainy day, then it was gone. It was weird. It made me sit in the sun for the rest of the day waiting for that sensation to come back. When it did, it was more like, like the electricity you get when you know somebody is secretly attracted to you and they ain't half bad themselves. Got a hard on lasted three days. Fortunately my new groupies were in and of themselves medicinal arts.

The new album had four songs that four different politicians picked up to prove they were hip and conscious. The Religious Right picked *Onion Up Yours*, can you believe it? But the bass line drove you down a gnomic path and the lyrics wouldn't let you swing them one way to another. Lyrics were bad ass mofos that did your wife and looked you in the eye and said I'ma do you too. Right had been achin' for some muscle for years.

Canoli had a fit but I told him be cool. I didn't own the music. Nobody owned the music. It was a dove.

"Yeah, man, but this is what it sounds like when doves cry. Stupid politicians."

"Brother, they'll lodge onion so far up that ass they won't help but be exposed."

We studied with yogis. Secretly funded coups to get rid of African despots and get food to their people because, y'know, damn. Got to sit in on high-level policy talks about national healthcare and, let me tell you, that's some sticky air. Humid as a bastard with too much money and not enough hair.

I released the next album two months later. Called it *The Reinvention*. Thirty-six damn songs and not a single throwaway. Hailed by critics worldwide as the first ever Great American Novel set to music. I became so huge I became small. I could walk into restaurants without getting mobbed because anybody who truly listened to The Reinvention knew that fawning shit wasn't cool. Canoli even got to riff on that one, a few acoustic interludes tied in timbre to the theme. Again, teach a man to fish. He'd wanted to riff his whole life. I told him to go electric but he said no, he wanted to slow it down a little.

After he released his album, *Roadie of Doom*, we celebrated like crazy. Bono had done the rooftops; The Beatles had done the rooftops; even Lip Patrol had done the rooftops. But when me and Canoli did it we took it to the stars. To the stars. My red guitar and his tan acoustic on top of a squat parking garage, downtown Detroit. Why Detroit? Because something the little alien dudes put in the water there makes Detroit rock! Windsor across the water was pissing themselves because they couldn't see. Through the whole concert I picked up imagery from at least a hundred clones on the four-sided clog below, black dudes, business dudes, yuppie dudes, dick dudes, pussy girls and trampoline artistes, every one of them humping up on whosoever was in front of their pants because you don't get to watch your host being probed without developing a healthy taste for it yourself; and because everybody was groovin' anyway and I'd learned to play my jams as if I was fingering labial lips.

Trent Darcell brought the freaking sixties back.

I swear to God somebody got penetrated when I kicked in the slow jams. Hell, if I closed my eyes I wasn't sure if I was playing the guitar or my boner. All I knew was Detroit was about to experience the greatest orgasm it'd ever had two hours after this crowd dispersed.

Mogasm.

Detroit rock city.

Me and Canoli hung around the Westin Hotel lobby after that in these glass towers the people still call the Renaissance Center but the suits call the General Motors Headquarters. The car gods bought it, the car gods name it. Renaissance Center. I like it. Gleaming glass towers that look like glass spiders should live there, and at night, at night it's like being in space. A billion lights travel across it. A billion lights sit fixed. A billion lights wink off. If you're lucky you'll catch someone undressing after partying the night. There's another high-rise hotel directly across the street. God bless fake invisibility.

So we got bored, went to my room, left the lights out and perused one such angel in bra and jeans brush her hair, search her suitcases, and finally, finally, pop that clasp after fifteen minutes.

Breasts as supple as fresh doughnuts.

Wrote a song about her.

Then I threw it away.

It took six months for me to look my first clone right in the face.

He said he'd been wanting to reach me for some time but, y'know, wife, children, responsibilities.

It was David fucking Bowie. The Thin White Duke himself.

The coolest person on the planet.

Ziggy Jehovah Stardust.

We met at Pink's, signed enough autographs to buy a few minutes quiet time, and ate two of the most unhealthy, ambrosiatic hot dogs ever will be. By then the sun was setting. Smog refraction makes California sunsets kick the ass off anywhere.

"D'you know why they haven't mastered faster than light travel yet?" Bowie asked in that cool, clipped accent of his.

"Not a clue."

"Because it can't. Been proven how many times? I mean, it's why Einstein did all that bother with his relatives. Their ships don't travel faster than light. Too much distance. No distance in time though."

"Why'd they come here?"

Bowie smiled at me. "They never left." That one blue eye of his and that one dilated eye of his hid all kinds of secrets of the ages. This man hadn't written *Rock and Roll Suicide* for no reason.

I kinda hoped for some serious exposition but he just shook my hand and said, "Helluva album. Keep considering time, luv."

Keep considering time.

I told Canoli I was a clone that very night. He'd just finished restringing my guitar and had plunked himself in the studio to tune it. Canoli could've been a pope in another life. He had that kind of gravity. Told him the whole story, how I was really just a copy of a silly, trendy man.

Canoli scratched at that little piece of goatee directly under his lip, letting the universe swirl around his head before he flushed it all in with the black hole of thought.

"So we become these little grey fucks, huh?" He put his medicinal weed down. Wasn't sick but why wait to fight the odds? "You guys here to save the world?"

Don't be stupid. Of course he didn't believe me. Not like people believe in Krishna or Jesus. He was just smart enough to take a good look at the other side.

"Not all clones are stars, man," I told him.

He twanged the first of four chord progressions. I picked up his guitar, closed my eyes. I followed his jazz. Took a single hit off his weed. In a flash I'd analyzed it down to its chemical composition and realized why most people will never make the Dream Time: they're too afraid to go to sleep. Weed, Xoloft, Xanax—it won't take you there. Can't. What was it Bowie wrote?

Something about *Time taking a cigarette;* something about it putting it *in your mouth. You pull on a finger, then another finger, then cigarette. Something about the wall to wall is calling but you don't linger 'cause you forget.* Something about everybody being *rock and roll suicides.*

Next time I see Spock I've got some questions for his anthropology-major ass. Canoli wanted to know how we became grey shriveled fucks.

"You wanna call your next album *The Clone Wars*?" he said.

"Nah, been done."

Canoli did a change up I didn't see coming. I coughed a little bit. He stubbed out his weed. I smiled.

I strummed chaotic like a butterfly for a few, but I caught up.

"You be ready next time?" he asked me. So we both took it for granted that they were coming back for me at some point.

"Hell yeah."

I was armed with the wisdom of the ages.

How cool is that?

Bowie's song played on. Fame was in how you handled being alone.

"...just turn on with me 'cause you're wonderful. Oh, give me your hands. Wonderful..."

Give me your hands.

You're wonderful.

***

The thing about television is that nobody after a certain age should actually want to watch it. I mean, it's all written to be as non-taxing to the 14 year old mind as it can be. Should any grown person ever give a damn about the new fall season? Now maybe, just because there are natural lulls and voids in yours and my life, having 2 or 3 shows to watch on a regular weekly basis is all right, but how many cop shows, lawyer shows, medical shows, wacky attractive white folks in wacky relationships comedy shows, pseudo talent/reality/documentary shows, fat-people-are-people-too shows, let's watch-paint-dry-as-I-rent-my-house shows, and idiotic news does the human brain need? And they're all the same bloody show!

"Tooth & Mouth: When it comes to crime, a crack team of dental technicians find that truth...is often in the eye of the molar. Presented with limited commercial interruption by Colgate Chewing Floss; tonight on Fox."

TV does not care about your marriage, your kids, the goals you coulda, woulda, shoulda reached, or whether anybody in your family ever amounts to anything. If corporations have the same rights as individuals (get this, they do. Yeah, I know) then TV is the Pope. TV tells you when to wake up, when to take a leak, when to pay attention to your spouse, when to eat, when to go out, when to stay in, when to finally get things done...because, for a lot of us, our time is scheduled around something stupid on TV. I remember when TV was at least a gracious guest, going all the way to at times trying to be art.

Rod Serling was a god.

Swallow

He hated being called 'Magic Johnson' but Johnson Wafers loved the way the ratings rolled in. 'Have I No Shame' premiered Monday with a guaranteed two season run likely to stretch into even more. "Regurgitainment at its finest!" he'd pitched to the Advertisers Guild, whose left eyes, to a man and two women, all twitched due to Starbucks poisoning. "We're taking people off the street, asking what they'd do for large sums of money, then a month later secretly placing them in those exact same positions."

"Sounds like Punk'd."

"No, no, this shit's real. Guy says he'd suck off a retard for a million, guess what? Short bus and helmets right around the corner. Hey, I put money in the right hands I can get the Pope to double dip a nun."

"You're not going to kill anymore hobos are you?"

"Baby, that was last season." Johnson covered his forehead as though he had amnesia. "Last season doesn't exist...but don't tell me 'Death of a Hobo' didn't make each and every one of you come. Vanessa? You came. I know you. Admit it, you came, didn't you?"

She smiled. "A little bit."

"A little bit. America loves me." He dazzled the room. "And when I kill a hobo, America hates the hobo. Christian Right objected once only because editing didn't take him out pleading 'Dear God!'—and I fired the entire production team—but get this, I'm rehiring them as the cast of a new reality show of production fuck ups who fuck up major productions, real movies too, like that shit with the kid, the one showed her titty before she was seventeen."

"Pederast," someone offered.

"Yeah, fucking movie earned two billion worldwide. Pederast Two is slated for production. My secret fuckups will be there. Let me ask a question now: I know Vanessa's silks are wet, but is anybody going to tell me Monday night ratings of 68 percent didn't provide the jumping off point for the most satisfying sex of your lives? Your wives aren't limber anymore but don't tell me that the hookers were closed! Davis? Is Agricult in? Norbeane, commitment? Stuck & White is the biggest producer of shit we don't need. I'm practically delivering a third world country to you with money they have no idea what to do with. I need commitments from everybody in this room or I will shoot every last one of you gangsta style with the gun held sideways and everything." He produced the gun from his blazer pocket. The smiles on the faces reinforced his love of theatrics. "Two to the fucking head, I'm not playing," he said smiling. "And we're gonna do something completely new with advertising for this. Each show, only your brand. Ok? Means one week S & W gets to showcase every piece of shit they've got for a solid hour, every little subsidiary that nobody knows you own. Vanessa, I give you the Spring slot to hawk No Fat Chickz. Perfect time to get that diet shit out there. Yesterday's premiere was commercial free except for the subliminal shit. Imagine what that would have translated to," he told the room, training the gun on each as a pointer. "Did I not prove myself to you?"

"It's why we call you 'Magic Johnson'," cooed Vanessa.

"It's why my magic Johnson fits perfectly in every one of your holes." He made as if to unzip. "Who here wants to see me fuck Vanessa on the spot?"

Fernando Elliphon's hand went up.

"Fernando, you freaky bastard. Put your hand down. Pens, ladies and gentlemen: pick 'em up and write something down." There were cameras filming the entire pitch, hidden but capturing everything in perfect HD. Vanessa Del Rio (she got teased about that all the time) had the kind of body and fashion sense that tended to get blurred on TV. But not on Magic's new secret show. Johnson affected a crafty look. "Ok, we'll loosen things up a bit." He nodded Fernando's way. "You hold Vanessa down while I fuck her and you commit to two as yet unproduced series. Sole sponsor." He proposed something equally outrageous to the other seven, coming around to something of a consensus on what they'd do to see that these deals got sealed. "Vanessa, apparently everybody wants to see you get fucked."

She just smiled at him. Vanessa Del Rio had devoured so many men in her life a protein cookbook was in the works.

She stood and shimmied her thong loose.

First up was Magic, then Gordon, then Elliphon and Epstein in tandem, then—after a bit more cajoling—Ms. Riggs from FreeMart. By the time Mailer and Pratchett hit it, Vanessa was more than just a shadow of her porn actress' namesake. She epitomized the dirtiest fuck in the world, full of sex and lust and hunger and teeth, with sweat, semen and labial juices across her forehead, cheeks and hair. Her diet company had every food manufacturer in the world by the balls. Del Rio said don't eat it, it didn't get ate. True power is the ability to fuck in a boardroom without a care about the world. Cameras captured her holding a dick in each hand and throwing her head back like a warrior princess before the final battle.

Ye gods, the season finale was going to be a helluva show.

Description in A-Sharp of A Beautiful Girl Whom I Will Most Likely Never Meet (or: Exorcism in the Key of Be)

Very similar to a song sung slightly off key by a man who's dreaming, conjuring and predicting through the veil of loneliness confused Muses have thrown into his eyes. Muses which force him (who in certain dreams becomes her) to confront the glaring white fields of chaos and fashion for them the explanations of things. They are like children, which is just as well. It affords him a sigh of relief they won't immediately see through his high-thrown hopes and prayers.

This is as personal as it may ever get because reality has forced its dreams on him. He chews the inside of his left cheek and stares at existence, rather rudely, for when it notices him he doesn't look away. Stares off within a sphere of (what is it called, so pert and quaint?) *personal space*. Personal space. Inner space. The final frontier. His name is Simon Templar, just like the Saint's of that old TV show. Those old stories. He is a thief and liar, noble and honest in his vocation. He knows one day he will be married. The world is full of foolish people and poor decisions. He longs for simplicity. Wife. Friend. Home. Happiness. There certainly must be a reserved space of time and place for these. Somewhere in the future.

"There are places you'll never see. They exist only within me. No one there is free. Because it's my reality."

The stigma associated with a (and again, what is it called?) *tortured soul* precludes and denies those who whisper from all angles, "We need to help you; here, receive the normal life." What makes their lives so easy, he wonders, disregarding obvious answers, that his should be thought of as tortured and difficult? They called him an artist. How he hated the convenience of that word. Artist! Difficult! Perhaps quite strange but certainly unusual.

Jimi Hendrix was an artist. He died trying to face the strain. Died young.

Simon Templar, the above by way of explanation, knew he couldn't possibly have much longer to go; if he was going to dream it'd have to be quick and constantly, using whatever, whichever, whyever and whoever was available before his time ran out. Which to those outside made him appear unable to commit, unprepared to acknowledge that level of seriousness which human emotions were due if they were to mean anything. From woman to woman he seemed to go, although to any who'd have bothered to follow they'd have seen he went nowhere, and thus "womanizer" was hardly earned, accurate—and to be honest—more than a little embarrassing. Failed expectations and subtle damnations.

Thus it should be known that every artist's greatest dream is of a beach to walk on, a home with a yard, buying forks and spoons, and sharing a meal hands to mouth without being afraid to smile. Which is of course far less than the impossible dream. Foolishness—no, not that; takes very little imagination to be foolish, and even less thought. *Folly*, much better, should also be known to be a necessary necessity, crucial in maintaining any semblance of life in one's daily motions.

"God help me! I love it so! I am not looking for *love*. Love is everywhere. Who needs look for it? There're over six billion kinds of it floating around all over this globe! What I'm after is ROMANCE in all caps. Talk to me, dance with me, trust me with a secret—Just allow me to gaze at you. I'll make a wish."

Somewhere in the future the wish will be. Not certain who she is but her essence remains the same.

You are cordially invited to attend the most joyous celebration this century has to offer. The marriage of damn lucky Simon Templar to (your name here), *to take place October twenty-seventh, 2310, 6:30 p.m., on the easternmost tip of K'laui beach. Attire of choice. No gifts allowed. If you want to smile feel free.*

Could be you. Or you. But it's definitely her. Up there ahead. The indistinct one. Yeah, that one, the collage. The knockout stream of sensory input.

Who would he marry? Given the go it's a good bet he'd have married the old high school sweetheart. Which leads inexorably to divorce.

He scribbles: "Expect I'd divorce and remarry after the bitter aftershock faded. While I am searching for the 'perfect love,' that which survives, I am also quite aware that I need another drink, nor will I find it, or would not recognize it if I found it--" and with every word tacks a Muse upon the wall, until the walls of his mind are completely lined and the Muses see all that goes on within and stop their baffled frowning, content for a moment but absolutely no longer. "So yes, I will remarry should another beautiful, intelligent, creative, responsible, indulgent, thinking, creamy kind of dreamy babe happen to think it's cool. Oh, and she simply *must* know how to properly appreciate a funky beat. Not watered down, weak funk, not no-talent divas, not the latest piece of bland R&B pap, nor the top 40 radio stagnation rotation. It must be uncut funk. Funk is transcendental, just as is the Rock. Gimme funk/rock and there's a good bet that I will make love to you in the farthest flungest reaches of group mind."

And now it comes to the fact that he was not thinking of the sea. The sea is a poem containing living rainbows. He was hardly a poem. He was a funky, cruddy beast, all grey and near dead. His thoughts were of a flower which was dying in a slim white vase she'd loaned him months ago. It might have been a carnation, memory's unclear, might have been pink.

Metaphors were everywhere, even down to the bag of two-day-old sunflower seeds he coddled in his lap. Both left and right corners of it had been opened, respectively he'd torn open the right and she (equals gone equals heavy equals forever) the left. He was commenting aloud to himself on the differences between them in an act so insignificant as the opening of a small bag of seeds. Her side was clean and precise; his was just a big rip.

He was not thinking of the sea.

So why then should the sensations of a beach possess him? A slow transformation from the heaviness of grey to the (if he might steal time from Kundera) UNBEARABLE LIGHTNESS of the deep blue sea. He was the water seeping with rhythm into already moist sand, and he was sound: the calls of gulls skip-flying atop the sand, leaving shell-like prints to mark their flirtations with the earth. He was froth on someone's toes. Those feet left prints as well, a single set weaving out and in with the surf. They were his. He tried to shake these sensations off because they felt bone-crushingly lonely. But the damage was done and pretty quickly melancholic lamentations wafted throughout all conscious lands.

Well. . . He could start singing Michael Jackson songs and find himself in need of tissue, y'know, like, *She's out of my liiiiife...* (sniffle). *Out of my—*

Bullshit.

Louder, say it. 'Cause ther ain't no wasy (Look, can't spell. Whoa, is this a sign or what?! Always happens when the game's afoot. A ray. Of truth.)

Consider him guilty.

"Do you understand, sir, the import of this trial?"

"Sir, I do not," came his reply.

"Witches are a fancy. What say you to that?"

Templar's grin: "I'd have to agree there," he answers, picturing her laughing silhouette. She danced upon the wharf in the night and shined brighter than the Northern Star.

"It is the impression of we assembled that you make light, heretic."

"Bloody objection! He's already got me guilty!" protests Templar. Unmoved craggy faces stared down on him like stone in high places. He glanced at each fop's face in their balcony roost. "I see," he says.

"Do you? Pray tell us, what do you see?"

"I could've done things the primal male but I didn't. Could've done it through a gauzy haze. But I didn't. The opportunity was there but I. Did. Not. Do. It."

"We've witnesses."

"Look, maybe I wanted to, OK, and Heaven knows I've been held sway by temptation more than once, but in this case I swear my innocence!"

"Yer lying through yer teeth!"

"All right! Maybe I am! You're of flesh and bone, man, how can you blame me? You weren't there, you don't know..."

"You admit your crime," the foppish barrister sniffed.

"I admit nothing. And further state that no crime has been committed. I concede to the dreams, but have you yourself not dreamt? Have you not known the stabbing pangs which fuel all life? Do you not know how often a man is driven by thoughts of all things female? You've not even faced me with a binding motive! Motivation? Her simple existence alone is motivation, and if we're to go by that then I should definitely have some company on this stand. Oh, you hypocrites. You fearful heathen. Sin just short of selling your souls and still think you're fit for saving. Have you never known a sensuality so seductive that sex was an afterthought to orgasm? I'm talking about more than temptation. I'm talking about, I'm talking about, yes, you understand, the airy feeling you get behind your eyes that's always a sigh or the cusp of a thigh—"

The fop tried to assert himself, having lost a measure of control, which fact did little for his consternation, beginning, "I hardly—"

"Definitely moving towards something, do you mind! Risk, ladies and gentlemen, take that risk even if you've got to whittle it down to its most nominal before you do so. You've already pegged me as a heretic so I'll prophesy this much for you: I've seen the future and it will be *long*. Pack a lunch. But there are no guarantees. So much beauty but that doesn't mean love. And love doesn't mean last. Ah, but lips are a joy especially when their little corners turn up, which forces the eyes and cheeks to light up, and just seeing that sight fills all the shadows with such a powerful glow that you have to restrain yourself from jeopardizing that joy. Gentlemen, if you're wanting a crime then I present you with this: she smiled at me and I dared think of kissing her—yes, merely a smile. Simple yet eloquent and always close to something wonderful. As for the other, she's no more a witch than I am a saint, and I should be more suspect had I not been seized heart and soul to commit that rash fancy. There's the more cause for worry. That was all to it; just a kiss. On the cheek, for God's sake. The rest I swear I know nothing about."

"You swear that was the extent of it?"

"Am I to be held guilty, sir, for what goes on in my mind?" Templar asks wearily.

The Muses clapped. When that wasn't enough they rose to their feet. White and red roses rained about him center stage. Sweat dripped from his forehead from the exertions of the play and unbeknownst to the cheering throng he wished they'd bloody well sit down so he could get out from under that damned spotlight and head for solitude. Go somewhere and think about the trivia of circumstance. Templar looked off to the side, moving only his eyes, to see the stage manager enthusiastically giving the signal for encore. What more was there to do!? Mephistopheles was not his name; he had no more tales to tell. He could dredge up this or that but surely they'd seen it all before?

Then the idea hit. After the curtain fell Templar motioned the prop man to his side and instructed him to gather together a perfectly mathematical white board, one inch thick by three feet wide by nine feet long, some paints, and a stark black tripod.

When the curtain rose to a hush the stage was clear of everything save the performer, who stood just outside of the spotlight's circle as if waiting. As if not quite ready. A second spot then shot through the darkened theatre, landing in the wings, stage left, illuminating the frightened prop man, signal that he should move. He wheeled the tripod across the lonely stage, the spot on him and him alone the whole way, Simon Templar still off in the darkness, and when he reached the midpoint between stage left and Templar he stopped and stood to one side of the board, revealing the multi-colored message painted across its length:

THE VERY FINAL DREAM. THE ROOM CLEARS AFTER THIS ONE.

The spotlight stayed on the sign. The prop man walked to the front of the stage, climbed down into the orchestra pit, went up the steps to the right, then walked straight up the center aisle all the way to the theatre doors, which he opened, stepped through, and closed without once uttering a sound.

"Or perhaps as part of a design," Simon Templar said when the click of the doors faded, his voice carrying through the hush. He did not step into the light; rather, the light moved to envelop him. "Fancied I'd be devastating, and prithee listen, I was. Fancied a song. Or even a Bogart send off for some future goodbye. Me with my roguish grin and soulful eyes, her with her heart in hand and a stiff upper lip. No rampant, rhapsodic emotionalism. Just a touch of honesty behind whatever words there were. Fog would roll in through an open window. The lights would be dim. Inside I'd be screaming, *'I could make you happy every goddamn single day of your life!'* but on the outside she'd hear something wistful, something unthreatening and meaningless: *'We'll always have Paris,'* he said. His hand wavered, hesitant. Should he touch her?" asked Templar of the audience. "Would she know what that touch meant? But there, it was done. The back of a finger brushed against her cheek. It moved—" His hand fluttered to his chin and stroked lovingly—"to her chin and rested a second as if it meant to linger. Too soon it was gone. And all the while her eyes had been on him though he could not (though he burned to!) look into hers. *'C'est la vie,'* she answers. Around them, out the window, a slow rain mists."

His hands had moved to caress one another without actually touching, more like caressing the air contoured between them. This was done intensely and feverishly, always a different motion, a different position, a varying speed, single-minded, self-centered—his breathing became quicker and quicker, sweat again trickled his brow—so absorbed and delicious, and... and...

"Oh, God! I see stars!"

The audience jumped.

"It's full of stars. That's what I told her but she didn't quite understand. You've got to have patience if you're going to count the stars. I told them that. Why the fuck didn't they understand!? Why walk away looking over your shoulder like I was a stranger, convincing yourself that a stranger's tears are nothing but water? I wish I was a whirlwind so I could smash up my room and be unafraid of the true function of anger. Oh, like a vessel I burst; like a vampire I thirst, Oh, definitely moving towards something. Landing flaps are down and I must ask you to remain awake until the aircraft has come to a complete stop. Now it can be told: the meaning not *Of* but *IN* life.

"I watched a man once beating himself with a stick. He had no clothes on. This was in a lavatory. This wasn't very long after I'd ended something quite unique with the only one who fascinated me, so I wasn't very tolerant. I took the stick away and broke it. He looked at me as though I'd dared slap him. He was crying. Trapped like amber in each tear I saw the tiny image of what he had lost: his wife to the dreaded disease indifference. *'Well, you get no sympathy from me, mister, and I'm damn well not going to take responsibility for you. Get your ass dressed.'* As he fumbled about I told him to stop acting like there's no tomorrow; Use his pain and sorrow to fill him up with power. Jabbing him in the chest with my finger I said, 'If you're going to partake of it then herein's the sweet and sour, herein's the only worthwhile endeavor. The heart. The beat of the heart, mister. If you want punishment just count the beats, 'cause it's ticking down and life doesn't get any more painful than that.' He started asking me stupid questions and I asked him just what his name was. He said Picasso. Might've been Van Gogh. *'What's it all for?'* he says, *'What does it mean that I am here?'*

"'Art is in the doing of the thing, not the thing itself! Hell, man, even I know that. It is not something to be discussed or imparted, not something to be explained. Why else an artist demurs if a work is praised? He knows that the important part has been done, that the artistry in the work has been selfishly consumed. What's it all for? Well, hell, asshole, it's for you!' And I kicked him out of the lavatory for interfering with me pee."

Templar stepped out of the one spotlight, which remained lit but did not follow, and went to the sign on its tripod. Standing in front of it, arms akimbo, the dreaming man's shadow fell across the quickly written directive.

"I suppose you can't separate one from the other. Like juggling, isn't it? They think you're juggling three balls when you've only got one. Love is God. God is love. Art is life. Aye. Love's more sweet than sour, nothing weird about that, even if, damn, you don't even know my name. Even if she can think up at any impromptu moment a thousand reasons to be contrary, or why flowers shouldn't be picked, or why sugar shouldn't be licked...or why, why, Why must I be the one you run to? I don't know but I, I think I—" He gave a little twirl and soft shoe. "Can dance if I want to. Oh, to be able to dance. To express with body as mind. Wonderful! To twirl and shake and fall and slide and twist and glide, all with you in my arms anticipating my every move. Dancers fascinate me, the ones who create. I like watching them. Emotion is art. Art is emotion. Ability to feel is the greatest gift humankind has to offer humanity. Dance with me into the essential void, the light fantastic. Emotion through movement logically obtained. Dance with me—Oh. Wait." He stopped, dropping to his knees and seeming a little embarrassed.

"Look at the time. I *am* sorry but..." he paused, he shrugged, and the one spotlight went off. "I'm free." Then he dropped prostrate to the stage floor, below the light so that the Muses were left with nothing to look at but the large spot-lit sign on an otherwise darkened stage, very colorful but simply not that interesting that they would sit there for very long.

The very final dream. As if he expected them to believe that. Perhaps for now. Perhaps for the night. But there's always tomorrow. The room clears after this one.

Made in the USA
Charleston, SC
30 August 2014